Surely Oliver didn't think she was going to let him pick up where they'd left off? Thinking of that gave her heart an unruly and unwelcome flutter, and she crushed the memory of his lovemaking with ruthless vigour. So he was particularly good at it. So what? There were other things—like loyalty.

'I'm going home, putting my feet up and telling someone very important to me how much I love them.'

His mouth thinned. Good. He had misunderstood, as she had intended.

'OK. But we need to talk, Bron, because there's a lot we didn't say.'

'You're too late, Oliver.' Years too late.

Caroline Anderson's nursing career was brought to an abrupt halt by a back injury, but her interest in medical things led her to work first as a medical secretary, and then, after completing her teacher training, as a lecturer in medical office practice to trainee medical secretaries. In addition to writing, she also runs her own business from her home in rural Suffolk, where she lives with her husband, two daughters, mother and dog. RELATIVE ETHICS is her first Medical Romance.

RELATIVE ETHICS

BY

CAROLINE ANDERSON

MILLS & BOON LIMITED
ETON HOUSE   18–24 PARADISE ROAD
RICHMOND   SURREY   TW9 1SR

First published in Great Britain 1991
by Mills & Boon Limited

© Caroline Anderson 1991

Australian copyright 1991
Philippine copyright 1991
This edition 1991

ISBN 0 263 77456 2

Set in 10 on 12 pt Linotron Times
03-9111-51507
Typeset in Great Britain by Centracet, Cambridge
Made and printed in Great Britain

Thanks to Paul and Robin for their expertise,
Rhea and Deirdre for their faith, and my
family for their tolerance.

CHAPTER ONE

'How do I look?'

Elizabeth Jones glanced up at her daughter, and swallowed the lump in her throat. It was a big day for them all, but especially for Bron.

She forced herself to run her eye professionally and dispassionately over Bronwen's slim, neat figure, from the glowing tumble of shining dark hair cut into becoming layers, down over the clean lines of the navy suit-jacket which hid the soft curves of her daughter's slender figure and lent her an air of brisk efficiency, down the narrow navy skirt and the matching sheer tights to the neat navy pumps, and then back up again, to study the face, bravely confident and yet with a touch of uncertainty mirrored in the wide grey eyes.

'Perfect.' She cleared her throat, and tried again. 'Just right. You look approachable and yet efficient. Have some breakfast.'

Bronwen shook her head. 'No—oh, Mum, I couldn't eat a thing——'

'Bron, you can't start your first day without a single calorie inside you. Now sit down and do as you're told!'

'Bully,' Bron said softly, but she smiled and obeyed, struggling with a piece of toast and a cup of coffee.

'Livvy still asleep?' Her mother's gentle query brought a flush of guilt and anxiety to Bronwen's pale cheeks.

'I didn't like to wake her just to say goodbye. Oh, Mum, I'm sure she won't really be scarred for life if I go back to work, but somehow—I just feel so wicked——'

Her mother laid her hand gently over Bronwen's slim fingers, and squeezed reassuringly. 'Don't be silly—I went back to work, and you aren't exactly scarred for life. She won't go short of love, darling. Don't worry. We'll be fine together. Now get off to work before you're late.'

'I wasn't fifteen months old, and you only worked part-time. I suppose I can always hand in my notice if it doesn't work——'

'Over my dead body!' her mother chided. 'Without your work you're only half a person. You belong there, Bron. You need medicine—and medicine needs you.' She walked Bronwen to the door, and gave her a firm hug. 'Did I ever tell you how proud I am of you?'

'Oh, Mum—I love you!'

Eyes misting with emotion, feeling the same tingling dread and anticipation as she'd had on her first day on the wards, Bronwen started her car and drove carefully the three miles to the Audley Memorial Hospital.

A new day, and a new start. Another chapter in her life closed. She stifled a pang of regret and dragged her mind away from the memory of a pair of vivid blue eyes the colour of a Mediterranean dawn, burning with passionate intensity, and a gravelly voice saying over and over, 'I love you, Bron, I love you. . .'

Lies, all of it. Yet even so, she wouldn't change a thing. And damn it, she still loved him, even after all this time and knowing the way he had lied. And there was Livvy, bright, vivacious, her tumble of gold curls framing a smiling face, and those incredible long-lashed blue eyes she had inherited from her father. For the thousandth time, Bron wondered where he was and how he was—not that she ought to care, but somehow hearts tended to go their own way.

She parked in the area set aside for medical staff, using the plastic card Jim Harris had given her to raise the security gate, and, squaring her shoulders, made her way through the door marked 'Accident and Emergency'.

The smell hit her as she walked in, a sort of busy antiseptic smell composed of polish and institutional food and Hibitane, totally familiar and very reassuring. Her mother was right, this was where she belonged.

She walked on, past the doors marked 'Staff Only', round to the right, second door on the left. Here it was—Dr J E Harris. Drawing a deep breath, she rapped twice.

'Come in!'

She opened the door and did as she was bidden, smiling to herself at the huge man sprawled like a teddy-bear across the chair and desk. He grinned, covered the mouthpiece of the telephone with one large paw, and mouthed, 'Have a seat—won't be a tick.'

She perched on the edge of the desk while he terminated the call, and then dropped his feet to the floor and stood with surprising grace, coming out from behind the desk to wrap her hands warmly in his.

'Good to see you again, Bronwen. Welcome to the team. Come and get a cup of coffee and meet the others. They'll be glad to see you—we've been awfully pushed just recently. Hell of a weekend, I gather. Pile-up on the A45—holiday traffic, I suppose. I was sailing.'

'Very sensible,' she said with a wry smile, and he laughed and patted her shoulder.

'Nervous?'

She shrugged. 'A bit. It's been eighteen months. Dr Harris?'

'Call me Jim, Bronwen. What's the matter?'

She paused, unsure of how to word her unusual request. 'It may seem silly to you, but I'd rather the others didn't know about my daughter, if you don't mind. There's enough speculation about single women doctors without adding fuel to the fire. Of course, if you've already told them, it doesn't matter——'

'Tell 'em what you like, my dear. I've told them only that you're joining the department—frankly, we're so pushed they wouldn't care if you had three heads!'

'They would if I were a cannibal,' she said with a grin, and Jim Harris chuckled and opened the door.

'They'd probably line up to be nibbled by you. They're a miserable collection of rakes, by and large, but good doctors nevertheless. Just don't let them take themselves too seriously!'

He wheeled her down the corridor and into the staff lounge. Forewarned was forearmed, she thought as the two young men lolling in the chairs raised bleary faces to her and then stumbled to their feet, interest flickering in the sunken depths of their bloodshot eyes. How tired would they have to be before they failed to register a reasonable-looking woman? Bron wondered, and tried not to laugh at their enthusiasm as they squabbled amicably over who was giving her a cup of coffee.

It turned out to be academic because the loudspeaker on the wall squawked as they reached the coffee-pot, and they groaned and tossed a coin.

'See you later,' one of them grumbled, grabbing his white coat off a peg, and Jim waved at his retreating back.

'That was Steve Barnes. This——' he indicated the other doctor, who had forgotten about Bron's coffee and slumped back down in a chair '—is Mick O'Shea.' The loudspeaker squawked again, and Jim excused himself with a mild expletive and a muttered apology.

Bronwen crossed to the coffee-pot. 'Hello, Mick. I'm Bronwen Jones. Can I get you a coffee?'

The Irishman raised his head and stared through her for a second, then forced his eyes to focus. 'Thanks. That'd be great. What a bloody awful night!'

'Grim, was it?'

He nodded, and sat up to take his coffee from her, gulping it gratefully. 'So tell me, Bronwen, what's a pretty little slip of a thing like you doing in a hell-hole like this?'

Bronwen laughed. 'One, I am *not* a pretty little slip of a thing—I am at least three years older than you, *Dr* O'Shea—and I'm here to work, and two, it's not a hell-hole, it's a well-run, modern hospital in an idyllic setting.'

'Well, it sure feels like hell this morning, and as for your being a whatever it was I said you were, I reserve judgement—even if you're positively middle-aged!'

Bron shook her head and tried to look severe, but Mick's eyes were closing again and his half-finished coffee was taking a nose-dive down the front of his shirt.

She caught it in the nick of time and eased his fingers from the handle of the mug. Mick murmured something unintelligible, and slid further down the chair, out for the count.

Finishing her coffee, Bronwen made her way out of the staff-room and out into the corridor off which opened the treatment-rooms. Middle-aged, indeed! Sometimes she still felt eighteen, young, shy and innocent, and the world seemed a terrible place, full of people tempting her with lies and platitudes; she shook her head and pulled herself together as Steve Barnes came out of one of the treatment-rooms with a laughing nurse at his side.

'Ah, Dr Jones, I take it you got your coffee?' he said with a grin, and stuck out his hand. 'Steve Barnes, and this is Sister Hennessy—Kathleen.'

She shook the proffered hands, and introduced herself as Bronwen. 'I left Mick crashed out on the chairs in the staff-room—he looked all in.'

Steve shook his head. 'He had a bad night—lost two of his patients in the space of an hour. It's his first SHO job; he only started on A and E four weeks ago, and he hasn't got used to it yet.'

'Do we ever?' Kathleen asked drily, and Steve laughed shortly and without humour.

'Point taken. I'm going up to breakfast—I'll dig Mick out on my way. Nice to meet you, Bronwen.'

Kathleen gave Bron a steady look, and smiled. 'Welcome to the madhouse,' she murmured. 'Come with me and have a look round—have you worked in A and E before?'

'Yes, in Bristol, but not for eighteen months.'

Kathleen twitched back a curtain across a treatment-room door and folded a blanket on to the foot of the bed. 'This is where we treat the walking wounded,' she explained, and opened the door at the far end of the room. 'The cubicles are open to the waiting-room through a door, and through the curtained opening to the corridor, so that we have access from both sides. It means that seriously ill patients aren't treated or moved in view of the waiting area, which is a fantastic improvement on where I trained.'

She opened another door. 'This is the plaster-room, and X-ray is opposite, with Orthopaedics through there, so it's all very convenient. Surgical and Medical wards are the other way, Paediatrics upstairs, and Obs and Gynae are in another wing—quite a trek, but they tend to be admitted direct. And in here is the emergency treatment area for acute and cardiac cases. In our more pompous moments we call it the trauma unit! OK?'

Bronwen was quite definitely not OK. Confused, bombarded with facts, names, unfamiliar geography, and all on top of doubts about returning to work. She shook herself and straightened.

'Where do I leave my bag, and what about a white coat?' she asked.

'See Jim. He's in his office. Come and find me when you're all set up—and don't worry, you'll soon get back into it.'

She grinned and walked away with the quick, businesslike stride of the professional nurse, quiet and no-nonsense. Bron had warmed to her on sight, and knew instinctively that the sister would do everything in her power to help her settle in.

With a sigh of relief, she made her way to Jim Harris's office. Just as she was turning the corner, she heard a deep, masculine laugh that shocked her to her toes. It couldn't be! Bron gave herself a little mental shake. She really must stop doing this, seeing him and hearing him in every tall, fair man she had seen for the past two years. Nevertheless, as she rounded the corner, she couldn't prevent her eyes from scanning the corridor eagerly, nor could she prevent the ridiculous little stab of disappointment when he wasn't there.

Ten minutes later, equipped with a bleep, a white coat and a locker key, she found herself plunged in at the deep end with an elderly man suffering from chest pain and acute breathlessness. She listened to his chest, and smiled and chatted while she took a history and observed him.

'Do you find it easier to breathe sitting up? Yes, I thought you might. All right, Mr Davis, you just sit there like that for a minute or two and breathe nice and steadily through the oxygen mask, and I'll get someone down to look at you.'

She detailed a nurse to stay with him, and found Kathleen Hennessy checking dressings in one of the other cubicles.

'There's an elderly man in three with what looks like LVF, but he's in too much pain, and I don't like the sound of his chest. Can we get someone to look at him?'

'I'll get the consultant down.' Kathleen crossed to her desk and picked up the phone. 'Dr Marumba, please.'

Bron, her face troubled, went back to her patient. He was, if anything, even more distressed, but she was reluctant to give him anything before Dr Marumba saw him, so she checked his pulse again and found it light and fast. His skin was damp, and he was obviously deteriorating rapidly.

She stepped out into the corridor again and looked up and down for any sign of another doctor.

Kathleen came up to her. 'His wife's here—do you want to talk to her?'

Bron nodded. 'Yes—is there somewhere we can go?'

Kathleen showed her into the office and then moments later came back with a worried-looking woman in her late sixties.

'Mrs Davis? Is there anything you can tell me about how your husband's been feeling recently that might help us?'

'Oh, Doctor! He's been off for weeks—hasn't wanted his food, and he's never been a picky eater. Complained of his feet swelling, and feeling breathless, and yesterday he was sick again—then this morning I thought he was better, because he went out into the garden and picked some strawberries for breakfast. He's been in the garden a lot recently, that's how he's got that lovely tan, but he hasn't looked well, and the backache——'

Bronwen leapt up. 'Thank you, Mrs Davis. That's been most helpful. I'll get a nurse to take you back to the waiting-room.'

She all but ran back down the corridor to the treatment room.

She took the nurse to one side. 'How is he?'

The girl shrugged. 'Not good. Chest pain seems to be worse. I've put him on a monitor.'

'Thanks. Taken any bloods? I think we need a total chemistry and blood count. It might be his heart, but I'm putting my money on renal failure.'

'May one ask why?'

At the sound of the impeccable Oxford accent, Bronwen turned and looked up—and up.

'Dr Marumba?'

He clicked his heels and inclined his head with a slight smile. 'Call me Jesus. Everybody does. You were about to tell me. . .?'

While he ran gentle but thorough hands over the frail patient, Bron repeated the symptoms—nausea, vomiting, backache, breathlessness, oedema, chest pain, and also the all-over suntan—and then delivered the coup de grâce.

'He had strawberries for breakfast. Aren't they supposed to be very high in potassium?'

He arched an eloquent eyebrow. 'Clever girl. Well done. If it is renal failure, it may well have pushed him over the edge. Let's get him in and then we can dialyse him PDQ if necessary.'

He turned to the patient, and laid a reassuring hand on his shoulder. 'OK, Mr Davis, I think we'd better have you in for a closer look at your problem. We'll soon have you feeling better. I'll go and have a chat with your wife now, and she can come in and sit with you until we take you up.'

He tucked a hand in the crook of Bron's arm and gave her the benefit of a ten-megawatt smile that could well have been a monument to the success of some unknown orthodontist, but Bron would lay odds that the dentition, like the man, was totally without artifice.

'Let's get a coffee,' he said.

Bron's lips twitched into a grin. She'd bet he was a real heartbreaker. 'Good idea.' They walked down to Kathleen's desk and arranged for Mr Davis's transfer to ITU, then went into the staff-room.

While she poured the coffee, she studied Dr Marumba as he prowled around the room. He looks like an Olympic athlete, she thought, with that powerful build and those incredibly long legs. His ebony skin was in stark contrast to the gleaming white of his coat, and his eyes twinkled like jet. He took the proffered cup and that smile broke out again on his face, lighting up the corners of the room with its brilliance.

'Tell me something,' Bron said, eyeing this delightful giant over the rim of her cup. 'Why Jesus?'

He raised a quizzical eyebrow. 'Apart from the miracles I perform? Because it's my name. True! They call the medical wards heaven—not usually in my hearing, and not usually in front of the patients—it's been known to upset them!'

He gave a rich chuckle, and drained his coffee. 'Back to the grind. I'll go and talk to Mrs Davis. Good to meet you, Bronwen, and well spotted, by the way. I'll catch up with you later.'

She nodded. 'Yes, OK. Thanks for coming down— he was my first patient. And come to think of it, if I don't get back out there, he could be my last!'

He laughed. 'You could always come and work for me if Harris throws you out!'

He gave a jaunty wave and left, and, setting her cup down, Bron followed him.

The rest of the morning passed in a whirlwind of minor cuts and bruises, sprains, simple fractures and a very straightforward case of a child who had swigged an unknown quantity out of a bottle of cough medicine, and obligingly vomited with the aid of a little ipecacuanha.

His mother was relieved and grateful, and marched the little terror out to wreak further havoc.

'I bet we see him again before too long!' Kathleen laughed, and Bron found herself smiling. So far, so good.

'All quiet now, Bron? Come on up for lunch, and meet some of the others.' Jim Harris dropped a friendly arm around her shoulders, and gave her an affectionate squeeze. 'How are you doing? Well done with that old boy—jolly good start. Marumba was very impressed. Clever of you to pick up on the strawberries. Here, dump your coat, forget reality for a while.'

He filled her in on the history of the building and the current state of the hospital as they went, and by the time they arrived at the staff dining-room she was totally lost again.

There was, predictably, a sea of new faces, all friendly and, she found, instantly disconnected from their names. I suppose I'll sort them all out in time, she thought, and concentrated on smiling and avoiding too many questions about her marital status and past medical career.

When they had finished eating, Jim led her through to the coffee-lounge and sat her down with her back to the door.

'Don't mind, do you? Only there's someone I want you to meet—you'll be bound to work with him fairly soon. General surgeon—excellent chap. Started here about a year ago. He was senior registrar at Guy's until then, and became a consultant at thirty-one. Meteoric rise, but he's extraordinarily gifted. Ah, talk of the devil——'

'As opposed to Jesus?' Bronwen quipped, but the laugh died in her throat as Jim rose to his feet.

'Oliver, I want you to meet my new registrar, Bronwen Jones. Bronwen, Oliver Henderson, boy-wonder of general surgery.'

In slow motion, frame by frame, Bronwen lifted her head and made herself meet the clear, steady gaze that had haunted her for almost two years—the longest, loneliest, most rewarding and challenging years of her life.

'Hello, Bron.' The voice like oiled sandpaper, deep and husky, rasped over her senses, leaving her nerve-endings raw.

She closed her eyes against the sensation, and felt the years slip away. . .

CHAPTER TWO

BRONWEN lifted her eyes and looked around the crowded conference room. There was no sign of Jane—typical! And there was that man again, propping up the wall with indolent grace: tall, well-built, a lock of his heavy gold-blond hair falling over his eyes so that he had to keep thrusting it back with his fingers.

Every time Bronwen looked up he was there, watching her with those startling blue eyes like a Mediterranean dawn, with a sultry promise of heat.

She shifted uncomfortably on her chair and cursed Jane for her absence. Where was she? He was watching her again.

She made a deliberate attempt to ignore him. It lasted perhaps fifteen seconds, and then her eyes were drawn back to his, tangling helplessly in that clear, bright gaze that seemed to dip into her soul. A slow, sensuous smile touched the corner of his mouth, and she blushed and looked away, more determined than ever to ignore him. Just a conference Lothario, she decided, and scoured the room for her colleague.

'Hi!' Jane came up behind her, and struggled inelegantly over the back of the seat, dropping into it with a plop. 'Just in time. Phew! What a scorcher. Have I missed anything?'

Bron smiled and shook her head. 'They haven't started. What kept you?'

Jane rolled her eyes and grinned wickedly. 'I met

this man—stunning. We're meeting him in the bar before supper tonight. He's here with a friend, too—said so long as you weren't related to Count Dracula you'd be welcome to join us. I accepted for you—OK?'

Bron laughed. 'Do I get a choice?'

'Absolutely not. That's him over there——' She gave a little wave, and Bron looked across the room in time to see the man with the blue eyes smile and raise an eyebrow at her. 'Isn't he gorgeous?'

Bron's heart thumped heavily with disappointment. So Jane had snapped him up—the story of her life! God knows, she was used to it. 'What?'

'I said don't you just love the way his hair curls over his ears? And those melting brown eyes——'

'*Brown* eyes?'

'Mmm, like toffee. Gosh, I'm not sure I can wait for tonight.'

Bron glanced across the room again, and saw the tall, fair man in conversation with another man, equally good-looking, but dark-haired, and as she looked he raised his hand and waved.

Jane waggled her fingers at him, and grinned. 'That must be his friend. What a pair they make!'

'Mmm. Wolves always hunt in packs. I wouldn't care to trust either of them,' Bron muttered, but her eyes kept creeping back to him, and then flicking away when she was caught.

In the end she resolutely turned her back, but she could feel his eyes boring holes in her skull, and missed every second word of the lecture.

When it was over they went up to their rooms and showered and changed. As she was berating herself for her indecision, Jane tapped on the door and let herself in.

'Wear the blue silk,' she said decisively, and lifted it out of the wardrobe.

Bron threw her a withering look. 'I have no intention of getting myself raped. God only knows why I brought that thing. I shall wear the peach cotton dress—or the navy one with the sailor collar——'

'Wear the blue silk,' Jane repeated.

In answer Bron hung it up in the wardrobe and lifted out a soft peach-flowered cotton tea-dress, delicately pretty and absolutely demure. Jane made a sound of disgust, and Bronwen ignored her and finished her light make-up.

By the time they went down, Jane had admitted defeat and conceded that Bron did indeed look very attractive in the tea-dress.

'Probably worse. You look so damned feminine that even a dyed-in-the-wool misogynist would fall for you!'

Bron laughed. 'There's hope for the average doctor, then!'

As they reached the bottom of the sweeping stairs, the two men detached themselves from the bar and came across to meet them.

'Bron, I want you to meet Michael Grant. Michael, this is Bronwen Jones. I'm sorry, I don't know your friend's name——'

'Oliver—Oliver Henderson. Pleased to meet you—at last.'

As their hands touched, a shiver of awareness surged between them, and Bron stiffened, and then with a smile Oliver engulfed her hand with his long, slender fingers and held it firmly. Eyes locked, they stood frozen, tingling with awareness, until a hand waved between their faces snapped them out of the trance.

Bron gave a breathless little laugh. 'Hello, Oliver.'

Oliver's eyes danced with amusement, and he released her hand reluctantly. 'Hi,' he said softly. 'You're looking lovely. Shall we go and get a drink?'

They gravitated to the bar, and, while Michael and Oliver organised the drinks, she had an opportunity to observe him.

He was tall—a touch over six feet, she judged, although from five feet five it was hard to be specific— and that lovely hair like burnished gold brushed his collar at the back, thick and unruly. She clenched her hands, just in case she gave in to her urges and ran across the bar to thread her fingers through its softness.

Heavens, he was just a man, like any one of the dozens she saw every day at work—no, not quite like them, her body denied. No one else had ever—ever— made her feel so warm and womanly and wanted with just a simple compliment.

They returned with the drinks, and Oliver squeezed in beside her, brushing her knee with the hard length of his thigh. She tried to shift away, but there was nowhere to go and the movement only exaggerated the contact.

He laid his arm along the back of the banquette seat and grinned at her.

'Cosy, isn't it? Do you mind? We could go some- where quieter, if you like.'

Bronwen nearly choked. She was sure his comment was meant quite innocently, but her thoughts and his words were becoming inextricably entwined. She felt the blush coming before it reached her cheeks, and ducked her head forwards to hide it behind the fall of her hair.

His fingers eased it back and he smiled gently. 'You're lovely when you blush. I really didn't mean that the way it sounded.'

She glanced quickly at him, and offered a shy smile in return. 'I'm sorry, it must be the heat.'

'Do you want to go out for a walk?'

'Yes—oh, no! I mean——'

'Just a walk. Trust me.' His grin was mischievous but wholly straightforward, and his eyes were open and sincere. For some lunatic, unsound and intuitive reason, she did trust him.

'OK. It's too hot to eat yet anyway.'

They wandered through the grounds of the conference centre, down towards the little man-made lake, and paused on the bridge, elbows resting on the parapet, sipping their drinks and watching the baby ducks for a while in companionable silence.

'So what's a gorgeous young thing like you doing on a God-awful course like this?' he asked after a minute or two.

Bron laughed. 'Treatment of Trauma? I work in Accident and Emergency. I'm an SHO, but I've been offered the registrar's job in December when she takes maternity leave. What about you?'

'I'm in general surgery. I found A and E too traumatic—literally.'

'Really?' Bronwen eyed him in amazement. 'I love it.'

'You must be addicted to your own adrenalin, then! I like the nice, sedate pace of the theatre. I can cope with that. You don't often get two patients at once!'

Bronwen studied him openly. 'You ought to be able to cope at your age,' she teased. 'How old are you— thirty, thirty-one?'

He chuckled. 'Not bad. I'm thirty next week. What about you?'

She smiled. 'You aren't supposed to ask a lady that question!'

'But?'

'Twenty-seven.' Her smile tilted her lips a little further.

He touched his finger to the corner of her mouth. 'Lovely. . .' His eyes fastened on her lips, and she moistened them involuntarily with her tongue.

He ran the fingertip across her lower lip, the damp skin dragging gently.

'If we stay here much longer, little lady,' he whispered, 'I'm going to kiss that delectable mouth.'

Bron felt his breath fan gently across her face, and her lips parted on a sigh of regret. She wished he would. Her eyes fluttered closed while she dealt with the storm of feeling suddenly raging in her breast. Who was he? Why this crazy urge to bury her face against his broad, firm chest and hug him close?

His palms cupped her face, and she sensed rather than felt his lips brush lightly over hers, once, twice, before his lips came down firmly over hers with a sweet, aching tenderness far more intimate than passion would have been. With a tortured groan, he folded her into his arms and held her tight.

'Oliver?'

'Shh. Don't say anything. Just let me hold you.'

They stood there, arms wrapped round each other, absorbing the warmth and humanity of the contact while their tumbling emotions settled to a steady roar. Gradually his grip slackened, and Bron stood away from him, raising puzzled eyes to his.

'What happened?'

His voice was gruff with emotion. 'I don't know, Bron. I've never felt anything like this before. It's as if——' He laughed, a little raggedly. 'My God, I'm normally so practical and down-to-earth! Perhaps we ought to go and eat—it's probably the hallucinogenic effects of hypoglycaemia.'

Bron laughed breathlessly. 'You could be right.'

Instinctively their fingers met and wound together as they walked slowly back to the conference centre, a large, sprawling country house dating from the turn of the century.

'Lovely, isn't it?' Bron sighed. She wondered what he had been going to say. It's as if—what? As if we were meant for each other? As if we've been waiting all our lives? Suddenly, she felt threatened by the short time they could have together. 'It's a shame we're only here for four days,' she blurted.

'Funny, I've been thinking that, but it's nothing to do with architecture and everything to do with a dark-haired sprite from the valleys——'

'I'm not from the valleys! It's only my name that's Welsh—and my father. I was born in London.'

'Poetic licence. Bron?'

'Mmm?'

He tugged her to a halt, and looked down into her face with eyes unguarded and vulnerable. He looked slightly embarrassed and very honest. 'I know we've only got a few days, but I want to see as much of you as I can. I don't know what's happening between us, I don't normally come on so strong. Whatever, there's something, and I want to find out what it is. No holds barred. I'm warning you, I want to make love to you, Bron, slowly, tenderly—I want to watch your eyes heavy with passion, your lips full and ripe from my kisses. . .not tonight, but soon. Maybe tomorrow, the next day? I want to know you first, but when I do——'

He flushed and turned away, obviously embarrassed. 'God, I'm sorry, I don't know why I'm rambling on like this. I feel like a raging adolescent—I'll be reciting poetry to you next!' He took a deep, ragged breath. 'There you are, though. That's how I feel. If you want to come along for the ride, the spacecraft leaves in thirty seconds. I should warn you, though. I think the pilot's gone slightly crazy.'

She gave a breathless little chuckle. There was a pulse beating heavily in her throat, and she felt unbearably moved and aroused by his honesty. She laid a hand reassuringly on his arm, and felt a shudder run through him. 'It's all right, Oliver. I understand.'

He turned back to her, his eyes searching. 'You do? I'm damned if I do. Look, if it isn't what you want, Bron, for whatever reason, then stop me now. Don't play with me.'

Bronwen swallowed with difficulty. 'Oh, Oliver. . . Are you serious?'

His eyes were steady on hers, and they softened with tenderness. 'I've never been more serious in my life. Do you want time to think about it?'

In answer, she stepped closer and, reaching up, pulled his face down to brush his lips with hers. 'I don't want to waste our time. I feel the same—and I'm terrified.'

He hugged her close, and the breath sagged out of his body with relief. 'Thank God!' he breathed, and then chuckled. 'Come on, little lady, let's go and eat before I do something very ungentlemanly and drag you off into the bushes!'

The crowd in the dining-room was thinning out by the time they arrived, and they took their salads out on to the terrace, eating with one hand while the fingers of the other were entwined.

After a while, Oliver gave up and pushed his plate away. 'I can't eat and hold you at the same time, and I daren't let go in case you vanish.'

Bron followed his lead. She really wasn't very hungry anyway. The feelings racing through her were nothing to do with low blood sugar and everything to do with the dancing blue eyes and the warm, generous mouth whose touch she had felt so briefly.

'I won't vanish,' she murmured.

'Promise?'

'Promise. Will you?'

'Vanish? No way. Where can I go? We're in outer space!'

They talked for hours, comparing likes and dislikes, hobbies and interests, and in the end they simply sat, their coffee growing cold, and stared into each other's eyes like moonstruck adolescents.

As the last rays of the evening sun dipped behind the trees, Jane and Michael came and joined them, and the spell was broken, or at least put on hold. Michael fetched fresh coffee and they chatted about the conference. Bron found it difficult to drag her eyes from

Oliver and concentrate on what they were all saying. In the end she gave up and closed her eyes, listening to the sound of his voice, headily conscious of the pressure of his thigh against hers. She wondered what tomorrow would bring.

'Time for bed,' she heard him say, and her eyes flew open in alarm.

He caught her surprised look before she could cover it, and smiled teasingly. 'I'll walk you to your room. Goodnight, Jane, Michael.'

He held her chair, and placed a warm and comfortable arm around her shoulders as they walked towards the stairs. Her arm slipped naturally around his waist and she felt the hard nudge of his hip against her side as they crossed the hallway and went up the stairs.

At the door to her room, she stopped in confusion. Did he expect her to let him in? She really felt as if she would, if he made the slightest move towards her, and yet it went so against her normal character that she felt a wild flutter of panic.

He turned her into his arms and tucked her head under his chin, the steady, even beat of his heart reassuring under her ear. His voice rumbled gently above her.

'I don't want to let you go, but I must. You're tired and so am I, and so much has happened. I want some time to absorb it, and I really ought to write up my notes on this evening's lecture.'

'Notes?' she whispered vaguely, and wondered how he could think of anything so totally prosaic while she was floating on a cloud of cotton-wool.

'Notes,' he said, more firmly. 'It's probably more effective than a cold shower.'

He released her gently, and, with a slow smile and the gentle pressure of his lips fleetingly on her forehead, he was gone, striding quietly down the landing. Bron watched the empty hall for minutes afterwards, hugging herself and smiling softly, then with a little laugh she let herself into her room and prepared for bed.

Oliver. She lay in bed turning over the events of the evening in her mind, hearing his voice again and seeing the way his cheek dimpled when he smiled, and the twitch of his firmly sculpted mouth.

It's all genetic, she told herself. He can't take any credit for the way he looks. Oh, lord, what have I promised him? With her thoughts in turmoil, and a mingled feeling of panic and trembling anticipation, she fell asleep.

'What we are talking about here is the Golden Hour, the time between admission and stabilisation for surgery in victims of severe trauma—for example, road-traffic accidents, burns, chemical leaks, explosions, et cetera.

'In the USA, and now in some fortunate areas of Britain, specialist Trauma Units exist, and they are specifically set up as emergency treatment centres for victims of such incidents. They have highly skilled staff available twenty-four hours a day, to provide specialist care instantly on admission. No fudging around wondering what the hell to do until the consultant has come back from lunch, or trying to phone another hospital to find out what the current treatment for chemical burns is—instant, immediate, accurate treatment within the first hour—the Golden Hour.'

The lecturer paused, and papers were handed out

down the rows. 'These are the statistics. I think you'll be as impressed as I was when I saw them. They outline quite clearly the importance of getting the right treatment within those crucial early minutes. OK, let's break for coffee to give you time to look at the figures. We'll meet back here in an hour to discuss anything you want to raise, so please don't waste your time— you aren't here to have fun!'

A laugh rippled round the conference, and the delegates stood and shuffled towards the coffee-lounge. Beside Bronwen, Oliver stretched and grinned. 'Hear that, little lady? We aren't here to have fun! Let's go and find a corner and look at his figures—although I'd much rather look at yours.'

'Oliver!' Bron blushed and laughed, and he grinned again.

'I'll be good,' he promised.

'I don't doubt it,' she muttered under her breath, and his startled grunt of laughter made her blush again. 'You weren't meant to hear that.'

'I'll bet! Come on, let's go and lie on the grass by the lake and study this lot.'

'I think we ought to stay here and concentrate.'

He gave an exaggerated sigh. 'If you insist. Let's go over the top. Michael! Grab two more coffees, there's a good lad. I'll find a space outside.'

Michael waved acknowledgement and turned back to Jane.

'Those two seem to have scored a hit with each other,' Bron commented, and Oliver shook his head.

'Just a holiday flirtation. I don't think either of them is taking it seriously.'

Their eyes met, and for a long moment Bron felt

herself drowning in the depths of those endlessly blue eyes, but then Oliver looked away and swore softly under his breath.

'What's wrong?'

'Wrong? Nothing. Everything's in perfect working order—it's just a little public to react quite so strongly to you, and when you look at me like that my body gets a mind of its own. Come on, let's go over there on the grass and sit down.'

He grabbed her arm and steered her quickly through the crowd, then they sank down on to the cool grass in the shade of a tree. He leaned against the trunk and studied her flushed cheeks with a reluctant smile twitching at the corners of his mouth.

'Sorry. I didn't mean to embarrass you. It's OK for girls, it doesn't show. You don't know how lucky you are. Hell, I thought by now I could control my reactions, but no one's ever got to me the way you do.'

'Oh, Oliver, don't apologise. You aren't the only one.'

Bron wrapped her arms around her knees to hide the hard jut of her nipples against the thin fabric of her dress, and looked out over the lake. 'Why is this happening to us?' she asked in a strained voice, and she felt his hand reach out and trace the line of her shoulder under the strap of her dress.

'I don't know. I can't think of a single thing I've done to deserve you, but I can't tell you how glad I am—hi, Michael. Drag up a blade of grass and join us.'

Bronwen looked up to find Jane watching her curiously. 'What did you think of the lecture?'

Jane raised an eyebrow. 'Excellent. Have you seen the figures?'

'We were just getting round to that,' Oliver put in, and Michael snorted with laughter.

'Bull! Right, grab a coffee and let's confer.'

Bron listened, putting in the odd comment, but content by and large to listen to Oliver's voice and to learn from his remarks. He was obviously very aware of current trends, and Bron was willing to bet that he was an excellent and conscientious doctor.

The conversation became more general, and she gathered that Michael was a senior registrar in the A and E department of Guy's, where Oliver was a surgical SR. She also learned that Oliver was waiting for the results of his FRCS exams, which he had completed recently.

'Hard?' she asked, and he raised his eyes to the sky.

'I'll say! I've never worked so hard in my life. They were killers. I don't think I stand a chance, but one can only try. The vivas were foul.'

'Rubbish. You can't fail. You've never got less than a first yet—bloody star student, this boy. Made the rest of us look as if we'd spent all our time in the bar——'

'I wonder why that was?' Oliver teased, deflecting Michael's praise. Yet another aspect of him that Bron found so appealing.

He unravelled his length and stood up, stretching his arms high above his head. A sliver of tanned, hair-scattered midriff peeked out under the hem of his shirt, and Bron dragged her eyes away from it and got to her feet, making a production of brushing the grass off her skirt to avoid his eye.

Jane attached herself firmly to Bronwen's side, said,

'We're just going to freshen up—save us a place,' and steered her through the bar towards the cloakroom.

There she took her comb out of her bag, dragged it through her hair and eyed Bron in the mirror.

'So what's with you two? You've been making sheep's eyes at each other ever since you met. What's going on?'

Bron shook her head in denial. 'Nothing. We just— I don't know. I've never met anyone like that before.'

'Well, I've certainly never seen you behave like this—the cool, calm, collected Dr Jones? Good grief, Bron, I always thought you were an iceberg, and yet if Oliver so much as looks at you I can see the smoke pouring off you both.'

Bron laughed. 'Is it that obvious? Sorry. We'll try to ignore each other.'

Jane shook her head vigorously. 'Uh-uh. Go for it— get it out of your system. I won't tell.'

'Sister Hardy, if you so much as *hint* to anyone that I've been behaving like a moonstruck teenager I'll get you transferred to orthopaedics—as a patient.'

Jane snorted. 'You and whose army? Come on. Let's go and tie the lecturer up in knots.'

In the event it was Oliver who had the lecturer tied up in knots, and the other delegates in stitches, but it was entirely good-natured, and resulted in an excellent discussion with much in the way of relevant contribution from many of the delegates.

By the time they broke for lunch, Bron was feeling light-hearted and cheerful, and they all took their salads out into the grounds and carried on the discussion.

Bron lay back in the cool grass and let the conversation wash over her. She was feeling intoxicated with the air and the sound of Oliver's voice, and she closed her eyes and drifted in and out of a light sleep.

She awoke slowly to awareness of him; he was lying beside her propped up on one elbow and watching her sleep, and she smiled lazily and shaded her eyes.

'Hi. Where are the others?'

'Hi yourself. Gone for a walk.'

He leaned over her, and his shoulders blocked out the sun. She watched, breathless, as his mouth came slowly down and brushed hers with careful deliberation. 'I've been wanting to do that for ages,' he whispered softly. His head came down again, and this time he deepened the kiss, his hand coming up to tangle in her hair.

When he lifted his head, his eyes were smoky with passion and he swallowed convulsively. He lifted a lock of her hair and wound it thoughtfully around one finger, then tugged it gently. 'I want to drag you off into my cave and make mad, passionate love to you, but the lecturer would be so disappointed if I wasn't there to stir things up.'

He laughed a little shakily, and as he lifted his hand to graze her cheek with his knuckles she noticed he was trembling.

'Oh, Oliver, I want you, too,' she whispered, and he gave a low groan and flopped back against the grass.

'What the hell are we going to do about it, Bron? I can't think, I can't concentrate; if I close my eyes all I see is your face. I didn't sleep a wink last night. I just want to hold you in my arms and talk to you—I don't really care if we make love or not. Hell, it's far too soon!' He groaned and rolled on to his stomach, burying his head in his arms. 'I never behave like this, and I can't believe you do either, but I have this overwhelming urge to take you to bed and make love to you until one of us begs for mercy! I'm just not sure I could cope with it yet.'

Bron took a deep breath. He was right, of course, she didn't behave like this and never had, either, but what they had was different, special, and she wasn't ready to let him go. She'd only had one affair before, and that was with someone she'd known for years. It had been a gentle and natural extension of their friendship and respect, and it had fizzled out just as naturally when he'd moved away for promotion; but, in terms of fireworks, already Oliver was winning hands down. If she let him go now, she knew she'd regret it for the rest of her life. When she spoke, her voice trembled slightly.

'I won't beg for mercy.'

He lifted his head and gazed at her seriously. 'Oh, Bron—I'm not interested in a quick roll in the hay.'

'Oh! That wasn't—I didn't mean. . .'

Her confusion must have shown in her face, because he pulled her into his arms and cradled her against his chest. 'I'm not saying I don't want to make love with you! I'm saying it's more than that. I think you could come to mean a great deal to me, very easily. I just don't want to blow my chances with you by pushing you into something you'll regret later.'

'I would never regret it,' she said quietly.

'You don't think you would, but things—people, circumstances—change. Come on, let's go back to the lecture and put things back into perspective. I don't think I trust myself to be alone with you when you're so vulnerable.'

'Oliver! I'm not vulnerable, I'm making a choice.'

He looked down at her, and shook his head. 'No, Bron, you have no choice. Where I'm concerned you're as vulnerable as I am with you. We're wide open to hurt, and we'll have to protect each other. God knows, I'll never forgive myself if I hurt you.'

He pulled her to her feet, and tucked her into his side for the walk back to the conference-room.

Jane and Michael were waiting for them, and they sat down just in time as the lecture began again. Bron made a conscious effort to listen, but it wasn't easy, and she caught Oliver's rueful grin more than once. He was obviously having the same trouble.

They broke for tea and stayed on the terrace with the others, and after the evening lecture they got together for a drink and a chat over the day's notes. Whether it was the atmosphere, or Oliver's presence, or just the fact that she wasn't used to it, Bron felt the drinks going to her head and found it harder than ever to concentrate on what they were saying.

Predictably her notes were sketchy and filled with doodles—her name and Oliver's, intertwined with love-hearts and arrows and trailing vine leaves. His were almost as bad, except that his doodles were restricted to 'She loves me, she loves me not', down the margin to the bottom line, ending with 'She loves me not'.

Bron took his notes, drew in another line and wrote, 'She loves me', on it, and handed it back, and he gave a startled laugh.

'Goodnight, all,' he said briefly, grabbed Bron by

the hand and towed her out through the french doors
into the garden.

'Just what are you trying to do to my blood-pressure?' he said with a ragged chuckle, and tugged her
into his arms to kiss her with all the pent-up emotions
of the day. 'Crazy girl,' he murmured eventually
against her hair, and held her, rocking her gently
against his chest while the nightingale sang in the wood
and the scent of orange blossom drifted round them in
the warm, evening air.

Then with a sigh he put her from him. 'Go on, go up
to bed while I can still let you go.' He brushed his lips
lightly across hers and, turning her round, he propelled
her gently towards the door. 'Goodnight, my darling.
Sleep tight. I'll see you for breakfast.'

On considerably reluctant feet, Bron forced herself
to walk away from him and upstairs.

The night was predictably sleepless; she lay, her
mind filled with thoughts of Oliver, and wondered if he
returned her love. How could he not? she thought
dreamily, and finally fell asleep as the sun crept over
the horizon.

She was woken abruptly by Oliver pounding on her
door.

'Bron? Open up, I've got something to show you!'

What on earth does he want? she wondered, and slid
out of bed, her hair tousled, face flushed, eyes half
shut. She caught a glimpse of herself on the way to the
door, and groaned. She looked a wreck!

'Come in,' she muttered, and shut the door again
behind him.

He swept her up in his arms and hugged her tight,
laughing with delight and something else. She heard

the crackle of paper, and then he dumped her on the bed and shoved a letter into her hand.

Sleepily, she pushed her fingers through her hair to lift it off her face, and dropped her eyes to the letter.

'Oh! You passed your FRCS! Congratulations, Mr Henderson!'

She flung her arms around him and squeezed him tight. 'That's fantastic! We'll have go to out tonight to celebrate. Oh, you clever man! Oh, well done, darling——'

His mouth came down hard on hers, and when he released her his face was blazing with pride and happiness.

'I can't believe it—all that and you, too. I'd better get out of here before I do something crazy. See you downstairs in ten minutes.'

He winked and left her, and she gathered her scattered wits and washed and dressed in double-quick time.

The day passed in a whirl of congratulations. Somehow they managed to make some sense of the lectures, but by this time both of them were relying more and more heavily on Jane and Michael to pass on relevant notes during their breaks.

The other delegates heard about Oliver's success and, not needing much of an excuse, decided to organise a party for that night.

Someone produced some disco lights, which were set up in the conference-room, and the chairs were cleared to leave space for dancing. The sound equipment was pressed into service, and a young SHO, who had done time on the hospital radio as a student, agreed to act as DJ. Jane dragged Bronwen upstairs.

'The blue silk,' she said firmly, thrusting Bron through her bedroom door. 'I'll be back in an hour, and you'd better be ready to blow their socks off!'

Bron laughed and shook her head in despair. 'OK, OK, the blue silk. See you later.'

Fifty-five minutes later there was a tap on the door. Bron was sitting at the dressing-table, clad in a tiny pair of midnight-blue silk panties and her make-up, toying with her hair.

'Come in,' she called, and she heard the door open and shut softly behind her. 'What do you think, Jane, down or up?'

'Down,' said a deep voice, and Bron leapt to her feet and spun round, clutching her arms to her chest.

'Oliver! What are you doing in here?' she squeaked.

He chuckled. 'Obeying orders. You said come in.' He walked towards her and, placing his warm hands on her bare shoulders, he kissed her lightly on the forehead. 'What are you wearing?'

'Not a lot! Get out so I can get dressed.'

He grinned. 'No way. Don't worry, I'm a doctor——'

'Huh! Anyway, you're just plain Mr now, Henderson, so you can take yourself off while I finish my preparations.'

'No. Is this the one?' He held up the mightnight-blue silk dress, and she nodded. 'Which way round does it go?'

'Oliver!' Bron tried to sound scandalised. 'It's backless!'

'Pity. I think it would look better the other way round——'

'Shut up and close your eyes. I'm getting cramp standing like this.'

'Your choice, not mine. Oh, well.' He sprawled out comfortably on the bed and shut his eyes. 'I'll give you ten seconds.'

It took her six.

'Right, pervert, do the zip up, please.'

There was a tap on the door, just as Oliver sat up and reached for the zip.

'Can I come in? Oh, sorry!'

'It's all right, Jane. He's just doing up the zip.'

'More's the pity——'

'*Oliver*!'

Jane smiled benignly. 'I'll see you two downstairs. Michael's in the bar running up the bill.'

'Whose?'

'Yours, I think!' Laughing at his horrified expression, Jane floated out of the room and closed the door.

'Do I detect a mean streak?' Bron murmured, and Oliver glowered at her.

'Mean? You don't know him when he gets going. By now, everyone down there will be celebrating my success at my expense, and what's more I'm not even there!'

Bron slipped on her pumps. 'Come on, then, what are we waiting for?'

'This,' he murmured, and drew her into his arms to kiss her gently. 'Have I ever told you,' he murmured, 'how very beautiful you are?'

'Oh, Oliver. . .' Bron coloured delicately at the softly voiced compliment.

'Oh, God, let's get out of here while we still can,' he groaned.

By the time they joined the others, the party was in full swing. They danced until Bron was breathless, and then propped up the parapet outside to cool off for a while before going back in again.

Oliver eyed her thoughtfully. 'How are we going to keep this going, Bron? I'm in London, you're in Bristol—it's going to be hell. Normal people could commute for the weekends, but the chances of us both getting a weekend off together must be remote in the extreme. We might have to wait weeks on end.'

She tried to smile. 'There's always the phone.'

He shook his head. 'It can't take the place of holding you in my arms—oh, God, Bron, I'm going to miss you so much!' He tugged her into his arms with a wild desperation that found an echo in Bronwen's heart, and she clung to him, suddenly terrified.

'We'll work something out—we must,' he murmured against her hair. After a moment he released her, captured her hand, and led her back on to the dance-floor.

In the middle of the evening the DJ paused to dedicate the party and the next number to Oliver. The song, predictably—considering that their blossoming romance was being avidly watched by all and sundry—was a slow, sultry number. Oliver opened his arms and Bron stepped into the warmth of his embrace with a delicious sense of inevitability.

He held her close, their thighs brushing with every slight movement, so that she was aware of the change in him almost as soon as he was. His warm, strong hands moved sensuously against the bare skin of her back, tracing the slender column of her spine and sending fire racing through her veins. His heart beneath her cheek quickened and beat more strongly, fanning the flames of her own desire, and when he led her wordlessly out on to the terrace to the other hall door and upstairs she followed without question.

At the door to her room she fumbled with the key so badly that he took it from her with hands only a little steadier than her own. Once in, he leaned back against the door and crushed her body against his, motionless for several minutes, then he eased her away from him and looked down into her eyes.

'Sorry, I just had to be alone with you. I couldn't hide my feelings any more.' His voice was gruff with passion, and yet tinged with uncertainty. He searched his eyes, and then his lids drifted shut and he swallowed unsteadily. 'Bron?'

'Oh, yes, Oliver. . .please?'

For a long, breathless moment, he was motionless, then he exhaled and reached round to slide the zip down with trembling fingers. Slowly, with infinite care, he lowered the dress from her shoulders until it slithered in a shimmering pool to her feet, and then he knelt and eased the tiny triangle of lace down over her trembling legs. With a feather-light kiss on the tangle of curls he had revealed, he straightened and stripped off his own clothes, casting them aside until he stood naked before her, the moonlight silvering the smooth planes of his body, casting shadows in the scatter of curls on his chest, darkening the skin to bronze. Her breath caught in her throat.

'You're beautiful. . .'

He gave a shaky little laugh that cracked in the middle. 'That's my line. Oh, Bron. . .'

He scooped her up in his arms and laid her tenderly

on the bed, coming down carefully beside her. She felt
the slight rasp of his hair-roughened thigh, and smelled
the warm, male, musky scent of his body as it joined
with hers, and a soft cry rose in her throat, mingling
with his as his mouth closed over her lips and captured
her words of love.

She hadn't known the highs could be so high. It was
as if a giant hand had lifted them and thrown them out
among the stars, to tumble gently back to earth in a
tangle of limbs and murmured promises.

Later, she lifted her hand and touched his face, and
found it wet with tears. He turned his lips into her
palm, and pressed a soft kiss on the skin. When he
lifted his head, she was stunned by the naked emotion
in his eyes. His voice was ragged.

'Dear God, Bron. . . I had no idea. Oh, darling,
hold me, I love you, Bron. I love you, I love you. . .'

When she woke in the morning, he was gone. He
had written 'I love you' on the mirror with her lipstick,
and there was a note on the dressing-table.

Gone back to clear up the chaos. Think it's best if
I sleep in my room—I don't want any speculation
about you. See you for breakfast. We have to talk—
there's so much to tell you. I love you. Oliver.

She showered and dressed and ran downstairs
eagerly, but as she reached the bottom step the manager crossed over to her.

'Oh, Dr Jones, I'm so glad I've caught you. Mr
Henderson asked me to give you a message. He was
called away in the night—awful business, his brother-
in-law was killed in a car accident. He had to dash
back; he said his wife—Clare, isn't it?—is pregnant,
and he had to be with her. Dr Jones, are you all right?'

CHAPTER THREE

'DR JONES? Bronwen? Are you all right?'

Bron lifted her shocked face to Jim Harris's startled eyes and nodded faintly.

'Yes—yes, I'm all right, Jim. Just a bit giddy. I think I stood up too fast.'

Oliver swore softly under his breath, and Bron felt her knees give way. She sat down abruptly before she fell.

'I'll get you a cup of coffee,' Jim mumbled, and turned on his heel. Out of the corner of her eye, Bron could see Oliver, his face composed, only a muscle twitching in his jaw giving him away.

He sat beside her and covered her hand with his. 'Bron? Are you OK? What happened?'

Was it her imagination, or was there a note of genuine concern in his voice? She snatched her hand away, but that only made matters worse because his hand then lay on her knee, and he made no attempt to remove it. Oh, lord, was she to be punished for that fatal attraction over and over again?

'Here, drink this——' Jim thrust a cup of coffee into her unsteady hands, and she tightened her fingers on the handle until her knuckles were white. 'Did you have any breakfast?'

She nodded. 'Yes, I was sat down and force-fed.'

'So it's not the hallucinogenic effect of hypoglycaemia?' Oliver murmured drily, and removed his hand from her knee. 'Just to be on the safe side, I'll get you a bar of chocolate.'

'Please don't bother,' she said curtly, and Jim looked from one to the other of them with puzzled eyes. 'Do you two know each other?'

'Yes.'

'No!'

'Yes, we do,' Oliver argued gently. 'We met on a conference on trauma, remember?'

How could she forget? It had been the most traumatic week of her life. 'Yes, we have met, but I wouldn't say I knew you—though I thought I did. . .'

'Bron?'

Jim's bleep went off then, so he excused himself with a worried look at his new registrar, and left the room.

'Just what did you mean by that?' Oliver asked.

Bron laughed, a thready, shaky little laugh that betrayed her tension. 'I would have thought it was obvious.'

'Not to me. Why didn't you reply to my letters?'

'Letters? What letters?' Bron couldn't quite meet his eye. There had been letters, three of them, addressed to her hospital, but not for two months, and by then she'd been so hurt that she'd thrown them away without reading them. And then nothing, just when she had been prepared to sink her principles and tell him that she was pregnant. She had wound up her courage to ring Guy's and tell him about Livvy when she was born, and she was told he had left. Mail would be forwarded, she was told, but they had no address as yet. Her courage had failed before she could post the letter, and afterwards she was glad it had.

He sighed heavily. 'I tried to contact you—several

times. When you didn't reply, I phoned the hospital and was told you had left with no forwarding address. I had to assume that what we had between us had meant nothing to you—but I was wrong, wasn't I? You're as shocked to see me as I am to see you——'

'Rubbish,' she got out, and he snorted.

'Look at you. If you aren't affected by seeing me again, why are you trying to throttle that cup?'

Surprised, Bron glanced down and made an immediate conscious effort to relax. The coffee slopped on to her skirt and she smacked the cup down on to the saucer with a defiant clatter. 'Damn—now look what you've made me do!'

Unruffled, Oliver produced a clean handkerchief from his pocket and blotted her skirt unnecessarily thoroughly.

'Thank you,' she muttered through tight lips, and he chuckled.

'Oh, Bron. Look, I have to go and start the afternoon list. What are you doing tonight?'

She closed her eyes. Surely he didn't think she was going to let him pick up where they left off? Thinking of that gave her heart an unruly and unwelcome flutter, and she crushed the memory of his lovemaking with ruthless vigour. Lovemaking, indeed! Sex. A juvenile exercise in relieving hormones. So he was particularly good at it. So what? There were other things—like loyalty.

'Going home, putting my feet up and telling someone very important to me how much I love them.'

His mouth thinned. Good. He had misunderstood, as she had intended.

'OK. But we need to talk, Bron, because there's a lot we didn't say.'

'You're too late, Oliver.' Years too late.

He stood up and sighed again, running his hand through his hair in that gesture she knew so well.

'Nevertheless—I left abruptly, without time to say half of the things I wanted to say to you, and I want to apologise.'

'So, you've apologised.' Her voice softened. 'I was sorry to hear about your brother-in-law. How was— Clare?'

'Devastated, but the baby's made a great deal of difference to her life, as you can imagine.'

Bron tried not to laugh. Oh, yes, she could imagine—only too well!

'What was it?' she asked, turning the knife.

'A boy—lovely, healthy little lad. She called him after Tom, but he looks just the way I did as a child. The Henderson genes must be very strong.'

She could imagine that, too. Livvy was the spitting image of her father, from that startlingly direct blue gaze to the unruly tumble of golden hair. She squeezed back the tears that threatened, and rose to her feet.

'I must get back to work. I'm glad Clare's OK and the baby was all right. I'll see you. . .'

She forced herself to walk away, and when she glanced back from the door she saw him watching her with a strangely unguarded expression in his eyes.

Oh, hell. That was all she needed. For two years she had told herself that he was an opportunist, an unscrupulous bastard—not her favourite word, she thought with a pang—but what if she was wrong?

No, she told herself firmly. Whether his feelings for

her had been genuine or not, he was married, and he jolly well should have made that clear and remained faithful, even if only in body.

But then you wouldn't have Livvy, her heart cried, and she closed her eyes and took a deep breath.

She opened them just as she hit the solid resistance of a muscular chest—a chest, furthermore, topped by an unforgettable smile.

'Oh! Hello, Jesus. Sorry about that, I was miles away.'

'Mmm. In hell, judging by the look of you. Jim said you had a funny turn at lunchtime. Is everything all right? You aren't pregnant or anything?'

She flushed. 'Why should I be pregnant?'

He laughed. 'Forgive me, that was presumptuous. I'm just hung up on it at the moment—my wife's about to produce our first, and I'm tuned in to the symptoms.'

Bron forced a smile through stiff lips. 'No, I—it was just a busy morning. How's Mr Davis?'

'Holding his own. You were quite right—his blood potassium levels were sky high, among other things. Pop up to ITU some time and see him. His wife's in there—I'm sure she'd like to thank you for your quick thinking.'

She nodded. 'Yes, I'll do that. I expect I'll see you later,' she called to his retreating figure, and he waved. She gave him the full benefit of her own brilliant smile just as Oliver turned the corner.

He scowled at her. 'He's married,' he snapped, and Bron gave a spurt of unruly, hysterical laughter.

'*And* with a pregnant wife. Don't worry, Oliver, Jesus is quite safe. I'd never knowingly come between a man and a wife, particularly not if there's a child involved. I don't believe in unfaithfulness.'

She glared at him and stalked away.

The afternoon was moderately busy, with a steady flow of minor sprains and fractures. By a quarter to five, Bron was feeling the strain of being on her feet all day, and was slouched in the staff-room nursing a cup of coffee when Kathleen popped her head round the door.

'A tummy-ache's just come in—kid of seven, vomiting, tender on right, slight temp—looks like a classic appendix. I've put him in three.'

Bron dumped the coffee-cup and crawled, groaning, to her feet. 'Lead on, Macduff,' she misquoted wearily.

She found the boy, just as Kathleen had said, suffering from acute appendicitis. He was feverish and unhappy, and Bron smoothed the hair back from his brow and smiled gently at him.

'Timmy, I'm just going to get someone down to look at you, so if you lie there for a few minutes we'll soon get you sorted out, my love.'

She led his mother out into the corridor.

'Appendix?' she asked, and Bron nodded with a sigh of relief. Thank God for a sensible mother.

'Yes, I'm afraid so, but he should be back with you by Thursday if they take it out today. I'll get the surgical registrar down to have a look, and we'll get him admitted. When did he last eat?'

'Yesterday, really. He left most of his breakfast, and I picked him up from school before lunch. I thought he was just getting a tummy-bug, because he was sick and complained of tummy-ache one day last week, as well, but he picked up over the weekend.'

Bron smiled. 'They always do the unexpected. Don't worry, he'll be in good hands.'

'You're very generous,' Oliver's voice came from behind her, and she jumped slightly and turned round.

'Oh! What are you doing here? I thought the surgical reg——'

Oliver shook his head. 'I've sent him home. He's been on all weekend and he's shattered. Let's have a look at your son, then, shall we?'

They all trooped into the treatment cubicle, and Oliver crouched down to the child's level and smiled at him. 'Hello, there, Tim. I'm Mr Henderson, and I'm going to have a look inside your tummy and take out the bit that's gone bad on you. OK?'

The boy frowned. 'Why aren't you a doctor?'

Oliver laughed, and Bron stepped in quickly. 'He is, Tim, but when doctors get *very* clever, they sometimes get to be called Mr again. Some of them, of course, get a little carried away when they celebrate,' she added under her breath, and Oliver shot her a black look.

His hands deftly and carefully palpated the boy's abdomen, and Bron watched in agony. How well she could remember the gentle and sensitive touch of those same hands. The memory still hurt.

'OK, when did he last eat anything?'

'Light breakfast,' Bron replied promptly, amazed that she could even speak.

'Drink?'

'Not since he got home at twelve,' his mother added, and Oliver nodded his satisfaction.

'Right, we'll give him twenty-five mg of Pethidine now for the pain and then get him up to Paediatrics and prep him, and I'll whip that little beastie out in no time.' He turned to the mother. 'Stay with him until we take him into Theatre, then I suggest you pop home and bring him in a few things. Would you like to stay overnight?'

'Oh, may I? He's never been away from home before.'

'Of course.' Oliver's warmth reached out and comforted the woman, and Bron bit her lip. She had known instinctively how good and kind he would be with patients and their relatives.

He left the cubicle and Bron followed.

'I think it would be better for my peace of mind and the patients' general health if you could avoid making crafty little asides like that while in their presence,' he said coldly. 'Anyway, I didn't notice you exactly holding back on the celebrating yourself!'

He walked away, leaving her stunned and miserable in the middle of the corridor. Mechanically she arranged for Tim's admission into the paediatric surgical ward, then handed over to her replacement and left the hospital.

'Mum? I'm home!' Bron wandered into the family room, and found the usual scatter of toys, but no one in. She glanced out into the garden, but there was no sign of them. It was a lovely evening and she thought her mother might have taken Livvy out for a walk in her buggy.

She sighed and picked up the toys. Had she done the right thing? For the first time, she didn't know where her daughter was or what she was doing, and she suppressed a crazy pang of jealousy of her mother.

She looked round the room where she had spent so

much time and so many happy hours with her daughter—Oliver's daughter—and a sob rose in her throat. Why, oh, why did he have to be working at the Audley Memorial? Why not Addenbrooke or the Norfolk and Norwich? Or, better still, right out of East Anglia—why not Edinburgh or New York or Sydney, where she would never have to see him or speak to him again, instead of bumping into him all the time all over the hospital and having to work with him?

Oh, God. Every day would be haunted by his presence, real or imagined. For two years she had wondered how she would feel if she saw him again, and now she knew. Awful. Far worse than she could have imagined. How was it that, after only three days, so long ago, she could still love him so much? She knew every little nuance of his facial expressions, the way the soft hairs grew on the backs of his strong, sensitive hands, how his voice softened and deepened with desire—oh, Bron, stop it!

If it had just been an affair, it would have been hard enough, but every time she came home, she would be welcomed by his child, and she didn't think she could leave every morning having kissed her little cherub goodbye and go in and face him as if nothing had ever happened.

'Hello, Bron!'

'Mummy!'

Bron crouched down as Livvy came barrelling across the floor and threw herself unsteadily into her mother's arms. 'Hello, darling! Had a lovely day with Granny?'

'Ducks!' she yelled excitedly, and squirmed out of Bronwen's arms to head for the stairs. 'Bath! Livvy ducks!'

Bron sighed and smiled. 'I'll do it, you must be bushed, Mum.'

Her mother smiled back. 'I'll make a cup of tea, then you can tell me all about your day, and who you've met.'

Huh! Bron thought. Get out of that!

In fact, by the time she had bathed Livvy and played with her for a while before tucking her, sweetly scented and rosy, into bed, there was very little time for her mother to drag anything out of Bron at all.

She ate the meal her mother had kept hot for her, drank four cups of tea, and dozed off in the middle of describing Jesus Marumba.

When her father came in from a late call, it was to find all three women of his household curled up asleep, the smallest in her cot, the other two on the chairs in the drawing-room.

'What a welcome,' he murmured fondly, and roused them to send them to bed.

For Bron, the rest of the week flew past. Tuesday was hectic due to a nasty pile-up on the A45, which had the effect of keeping Oliver in Theatre operating on the internal injuries, and Wednesday, although quiet in A and E, was his other list day, so he was similarly occupied.

Knowing he was securely out of the way, Bron popped up to Paediatrics to see little Tim, and found him recovering well after his appendicectomy.

'He's coming home tomorrow,' his mother told her with a smile. 'He's made a marvellous recovery, and it's such a neat little incision.'

'I'm glad he's so well,' Bron said warmly, and left

before the mother could launch into a litany of praise for the great man himself.

Thursday consisted of the general mish-mash of walking wounded needing running-repairs, and on Thursday night she was on call, spending her first night in the little room reserved for the purpose.

Not that she spent very much time in there asleep, and by Friday she felt as if she had been working in the department all her life.

Jim Harris was highly supportive, Kathleen was professional, conscientious and blessed with a dry wit that saved Bron from despair on more than one occasion, and Steve Barnes and Mick O'Shea were reliable and cheerful.

Jesus came to see her on Friday morning. 'Mr Davis sends you his love. I gather you've been up to see him once or twice—he said to tell you if you were thirty years older, or if he were thirty years younger, he wouldn't be saying goodbye! He's been transferred to Cambridge,' he told her. 'They've got a specialist renal unit up there. You know, we only got him in the nick of time. We had to bring the levels down very slowly; he'd obviously been in some degree of failure for ages. It'll take weeks to shift that oedema.'

'How's he taken it?'

Jesus shrugged. 'Very well. He's philosophical about needing dialysis, and his wife is busy boning up on the dietary requirements, so they seem to be tackling it head on.'

'No more strawberries, though. He'll miss them!'

Jesus laughed shortly. 'He'll just have to, I'm afraid. Well spotted, by the way. What made you think of it?'

'Ah! I have a friend whose brother is on CAPD—
you know, continuous——'

'Ambulatory peritoneal dialysis. Yes, I have heard
of it,' he commented drily. 'So you know all about the
dietary restrictions?'

'Enough to know that if it happens to me it's goodbye
to strawberries. Fancy, Wimbledon without
strawberries!'

'Anyone for tennis?'

Bron's heart turned over and flip-flopped for a
moment.

'Nice to see a serious medical discussion taking
place,' he added.

'Actually, Oliver, it was. Bronwen spotted a man in
renal failure heavily disguised as LVF on Monday, and
I was just updating her.'

Oliver arched a disbelieving brow and, continuing to
ignore Bron, asked Jesus pointedly how his wife was
doing.

With great enthusiasm, he launched into a blow-by-
blow account of the third trimester of her pregnancy,
and Bron left them to it with a private smile. That
would teach him to be so damn suspicious!

At lunchtime Jim collected her from the staff-room,
peeled off her coat and handed her her bleep.

'Come on, we're going to the pub. Friday tradition.
One of the perks of growing up is you get to sit in the
garden of the pub over the way and watch for the
ambulances over a glass of alcohol-free lager and a
prawn salad!'

Bron chuckled and picked up her jacket. 'OK.
Sounds good.'

But when they got there, her heart misbehaved again

because Oliver and Jesus Marumba were lounging comfortably on a teak seat in the shade of a tree.

'Hi!' Jesus stood and offered her his end of the seat, and Bron took it reluctantly. What else could she do without appearing churlish? Anyway, Oliver could have been gentlemanly and offered her his seat first, except of course that he wouldn't do that because she would have then been sitting next to Jesus—oh, what a ridiculous farce!

She made herself as small as possible and tried not to look at Oliver, but it was difficult, especially when Jesus was called away by his bleep and Jim was inside getting their drinks.

'So,' he said, to break the silence, 'how's it going?'

'Fine, thank you. I'm enjoying it, if that's the right word. Last night was my first on call—very busy, but I like that.' Not too much time to think about you, she added to herself.

'Yes, I remember you saying you loved A and E. What do you think of the Major Incident contingency plans?'

She looked at him then. 'Very good. They're your idea, aren't they?'

He nodded. 'Mine and Jim's—he's very hot on early trauma treatment. He's spent some time in the States studying it.'

Jim returned then and they discussed the subject at length. Oliver turned to her after a while and asked if she had been able to institute any changes in the A and E department she had worked in before.

'I—er—no, not really. I wasn't there for long enough.'

His brow creased into a frown. 'Why didn't you take the registrar's job?'

Bron improvised frantically. 'Well, that was the original idea, but then another opportunity presented itself and—my plans changed.'

Get me out of here, she prayed, and, as if in answer, her bleep sounded.

She grinned apologetically. 'Sorry, chaps. Catch up with you later.'

Almost dropping her glass back on to the table, she walked swiftly across the grass, ran down the steps and across the forecourt to A and E. Thank heavens for small mercies, she thought, but her reprieve was short-lived.

Her patient was a man in his late twenties, lying groaning with his hands clutching his abdomen. His wife was sitting with him and smoothing his brow, which was damp and clammy.

Peeling back the blanket, she quickly asked when the symptoms had first started.

His wife replied. 'He's been haymaking, lifting heavy bales. He's been complaining of backache for days, and then this dinnertime he came in looking awful. I didn't bother with the doctor, just called the ambulance.'

'Very sensible.' Bron ran her hands gently over his abdomen, and then straightened and replaced the blanket. 'Look, I'm going to get someone down to see him, but I think he's going to need an operation. I don't think it's anything to do with his back, I think it's a tummy problem. Just stay with him, could you? I'll be back in a tick.'

She went out and picked up the phone. 'Can you get

me Mr Henderson down to A and E please? Fast. He's got his bleep with him. Thanks.' She replaced the receiver. She had found a large mass in his abdomen, and she was worried. He was in shock, and his blood-pressure was low.

She was just checking it again when Oliver appeared. She followed him out.

'What's the problem?'

'BP eighty over forty, light, rapid pulse, respiration strained. Central abdominal pain, and there's a large mass in the mid-line. It feels like a tumour. He's been complaining of backache for weeks, apparently.'

Oliver frowned. 'Doesn't add up. That BP's too low. Sounds more like an aneurysm beginning to rupture, but he's far too young. I'm going to have a look. Kathleen, warn Theatre, we may want them fast. And I want his blood-pressure monitored continuously. What's his name?'

'Peter Griffiths.'

Oliver flicked the curtain aside and went in. 'Peter? How are you feeling now? Do you mind if I take a look at you?'

He peeled down the blanket and examined his abdomen thoroughly, talking reassuringly to the man all the time. 'Mmm. Peter, we need a closer look at this in Theatre, OK?'

The young man nodded slightly, and reached out his hand to his wife. 'Jill? Stay with me, love. It hurts like hell.'

She lifted panic-stricken eyes to Oliver, and he squeezed her shoulder reassuringly. 'We'll get rid of the pain, then sort him out. Do you think you could wait outside for a moment——?'

Just then her husband gave a low moan, clutched at his wife's hand and slid quietly into unconsciousness.

Oliver laid his hand on the man's abdomen and went absolutely still. By the time he straightened up, Bron had pumped up the blood-pressure cuff and was frantically trying to find his pulse.

Oliver called, 'Resus. team, please!' and elbowed Mrs Griffiths gently out of the way. A nurse appeared and removed her discreetly into the corridor, and the team sprang into action.

'ABC,' Bron muttered, and somehow her shaking hands inserted a Brooks airway.

'Right, get him some air. Let's have some atropine, calcium and adrenalin, please, Kathleen. We'll give him the lot—we've got nothing to lose. Can someone get in an IV line?' All the while he was talking, Oliver was working steadily on Peter Griffiths's chest, pumping rhythmically on the sternum, co-ordinating with the nurse who was working the airbag.

Bron got the IV line in and injected the drugs, and someone connected him up to the cardiac monitor, and switched it on. Immediately Oliver's head came up.

'Turn that bloody alarm off,' he muttered. 'We all know what's going on.'

He injected adrenalin directly into the young man's heart, but with no effect.

'I'm getting no reaction from the pupils,' Kathleen reported quietly, but they kept working, although there was no sign of life, until the sweat was dripping down Oliver's forehead and running into his eyes, and then he swore softly and straightened up, defeat in every line of his body.

'I'll take over,' Bron said frantically, and began to

pump his chest with new energy, but Oliver laid a hand over hers and shook his head briefly.

She stared at him in horror. 'No. . .?'

Oliver carefully and deliberately folded up his stethoscope and replaced it in his pocket, and then walked out into the corridor to the confused and shocked young woman sitting outside.

'Mrs Griffiths—Jill, I'm sorry. There's no easy way to tell you this——'

'Is he. . .he's not. . .?'

Oliver nodded. 'I'm afraid we lost him. I think he had a leaky blood vessel, and it just suddenly gave up. We did everything we could. I'll get someone to get you a cup of tea.'

She turned helpless eyes to Bron, and then looked past her at her husband. 'Could I have a minute with him? On my own?'

Oliver swallowed and raked his hand through his hair. 'Yes, of course.'

He put his arm around Bron and led her out and across to the staff-room. 'Stay here,' he said quietly, 'I'll be back in a minute.'

Bron closed her eyes and breathed deeply. Her first death. She supposed she had been lucky to escape it for a whole week, but she hated losing a patient. Especially such a young, apparently healthy man. The slow tears squeezed under her lids and she pressed her fist against her mouth to muffle the sob.

Oliver's arms closed round her and he rocked her gently against his chest. 'I won't insult your intelligence by telling you not to get involved. Just let it out.'

She sagged against him and let the tears come, and

then he blotted her up with a handful of tissues and pushed her into a chair.

'Drink this,' he ordered, coming back with a strong cup of coffee, and she noticed his hand was shaking.

'I thought it was a tumour,' she said, still shocked. 'How could I have missed that aneurysm? It must have been pulsating, but I didn't feel it——'

'Easy. You weren't looking for it in a man of twenty-eight. If it helps you, it wouldn't have made any difference to what you did, what I did or the eventual outcome. We still would have lost him. It must have been leaking for hours.'

'I wondered why his BP had dropped so much.'

She drank her coffee in silence, and when she looked up he was watching her with a strange expression on his face.

'Have I got a smudge on my nose?' she asked with a weak attempt at levity, and he smiled slightly and shook his head.

'I wondered if you were doing anything tomorrow. Clare and Tom aren't here this weekend, and I thought it might be nice to go to Cambridge and go punting on the river, or something.'

'Oliver, we can't!'

His jaw tensed. 'Why, are you busy?'

She thought of Livvy, who hadn't seen her mother all week, and her own parents, who would doubtless like a rest, and sighed regretfully.

'You could say that. And anyway, I don't think we should. Oliver, I don't want you to think you can crook your little finger and I'll fall into bed with you——'

He looked genuinely shocked. 'I wouldn't ask you to, Bron. I know we rushed things before, and I can understand that you might not want to have—that kind of a relationship with me. But is there any reason why we can't be friends?'

She thought of the wild beating of her heart every time she heard his voice, of his two children who knew nothing of each other's existence, of the way she could sense his presence in a room as if by radar. Friends? She could think of plenty of things they could be, but friends? Now there was a novel idea!

'I'd like that,' she heard herself say.

'Good.' He got to his feet. 'Look, forget Cambridge if you like. How about a walk tomorrow afternoon? Here's my number——' he scribbled on a scrap of paper and handed it to her '—ring me if you change your mind. I must go and talk to Mrs Griffiths again, then I've got to check my patients. Think about it, Bron. It would do you good.'

Somehow she doubted that, but she knew, whatever she decided, she would be thinking about it—and him—one way or the other, all weekend. After all, why should this weekend be any different?

She wasn't sure if it was because she genuinely wanted friendship with Oliver, or if it was because Peter Griffiths had been younger than her, but she suddenly felt that she ought to get to know him as well as she could. After all, he was Livvy's father, and she owed it to her daughter to be able to tell her, in later years, the kind of man her father was.

I'll ring him tomorrow, she thought, and go for a walk. After all, what harm can it do?

CHAPTER FOUR

BY THE morning, Bronwen was beset by doubts. Livvy was demanding and difficult, and was obviously developing a slight cold. She clung to Bron, whinging and miserable, and succeeded in reopening the Pandora's box of guilt that Bron thought she had managed to squeeze slowly shut during the week.

By midday the baby was over-tired and even more fretful, and Bron knew she couldn't leave her. Stifling her disappointment, she decided to ring Oliver and tell him she wouldn't be able to go, and consoled herself with all sorts of sensible remarks about letting sleeping tigers lie and such-like.

It didn't work. She was miserable. Oliver was out, and she rang twice just to listen to his voice on the answering-machine.

Deciding that what she had to say was too complicated for words, far less the impersonal medium of a recorded message, she hung up each time without saying anything.

Her mother eyed her speculatively, and then, after a snack lunch fraught with Livvy's temper and Bron's obvious exhaustion, Mrs Jones suggested that Livvy ought to go to bed and Bron ought to get out into the fresh air.

'Why don't you take the car and go out to the woods and have a good, long walk? It would pep you up— you look very peaky. I'll take care of Livvy. Go on.'

Oh, God! Even her mother was on Oliver's side. Livvy obligingly fell asleep as soon as her grandmother scooped her up from her high-chair, and while she was upstairs Bron tried Oliver again. He picked up the phone on the second ring, and Bron felt her mouth dry.

'Hello? Henderson here.' There was a pause, during which Bron frantically tried to make her throat work, and then he said 'Hello?' again, impatiently.

She finally got her vocal apparatus to co-operate—more or less. 'It's Bron. I thought—if you want—I'm going out for a walk, to the woods near here, but I expect you're too busy——'

'Bron, shut up,' he said fondly, and she subsided with a silly smile. 'Now, where are these woods?'

She gave him directions, arranged to meet him there as soon as he could get away, and ran to her bedroom to change her blouse. She pulled three out of the wardrobe, put them all back, and got out a shapeless and colourful T-shirt instead. She dragged a brush through her hair, looked in despair at her face, and tried to put a touch of colour on her lips. Her mother walked into the room and guilt made Bron jump, smudging the lipstick.

'Whatever are you doing? You don't need make-up to go for a walk!'

Bron avoided her mother's all-too-seeing eyes. 'You're right—I look ridiculous. I'll take it off.'

She scrubbed furiously at her lips and hated herself for the flags of guilty colour that flew in her cheeks.

'I never said you looked ridiculous—just that it was unnecessary for a walk in the woods.'

'I looked so pale,' she explained lamely, and caught her mother's sceptical glance.

'Bron,' her mother sighed, 'I've known you for a long time, and through a great deal. I would like to think I'm your friend as well as your mother. If you don't want to talk about it, don't, but please don't lie to me.'

Bron closed her eyes and propped her head on her hands, drawing in a shaky breath.

'Oliver's working at the hospital.'

Her mother's silence was broken by a heavy sigh. 'Oh, dear. I thought there was something wrong. How do you feel?'

She shrugged. 'Confused, ecstatic, miserable—I don't know! Oh, Mum, I thought it was just a crazy holiday romance, a momentary lapse, but it wasn't—I really do still love him.' She took a deep breath, and turned towards her mother. 'He's got a son, called Tom. He says he looks just like him. What do I do? I can't tell him about Livvy, I can't! How can I? It's as much my fault as his that I got pregnant, so I can't dump the blame on him. He doesn't deserve that burden. If his marriage is shaky, then Clare and Tom will suffer dreadfully, and if he'd leave them for me I'm not sure I'd want him anyway. What's to stop it happening all over again with someone else? But I still love him. How can I? I must be out of my mind. . .'

Her mother reached out and squeezed Bron's hand. 'Oh, darling, I'm so sorry. Do you have to work much with him?'

'Enough. He's one of the general surgical consultants. He's always hanging around A and E, and if he isn't there everyone's always singing his praises. It's impossible to ignore him, and he doesn't seem to want to leave me alone. That's one reason why I agreed to meet him this afternoon. I think we need to talk, sort this thing out between us, and see if we can't find some sort of neutral ground so that we can work together.'

Her mother nodded slowly. 'I agree. I think you've got to establish some ground-rules so that you both know where you stand—and I think you're absolutely right about Livvy. He would only want to meet her, and that won't help anyone. Wait and see—if you keep him at arm's length for long enough, he'll probably get bored and move on to pastures new, if he's that sort.'

'And if he isn't? What if his marriage has been unhappy for years, and he's only staying with Clare because of Tom? Doesn't Livvy deserve a father just as much? Oh, damn him!'

Bron burst into tears, and her mother folded her gently into her arms and rocked her as if she were a child until the storm had passed. Then she handed her a tissue, told her to wash her face and put on a little make-up and go and get it over with.

By the time Bron arrived, Oliver was parked in the picnic area she had told him about, and was leaning against his dark grey Mercedes with his arms folded and his legs crossed at the ankle. He was wearing worn, faded jeans that rode low on his slim hips and hugged his lean, well-muscled legs with loving familiarity, and an old soft grey cotton shirt was stretched taut across his shoulders, highlighting their breadth. The sleeves were rolled up to expose warmly tanned forearms dusted with gold hair that glinted in the sun, and Bron could see the curls at the base of his throat nestling in the open neck.

When he saw her, he shouldered himself away from the car and sauntered towards her with his long, lazy stride. Sleeping tigers, she thought and, swallowing against the rising tide of panic, she crashed the gears, finally engaging reverse and slotting the car into a space well away from his. When she looked up, he was standing safely to one side, a slight smile playing around the corners of his mouth.

He knows, she thought, damn it! He knows I'm in a frenzy and don't know how to cope. She fumbled for the door-handle just as he reached the door and opened it smoothly, stepping back out of her way.

She forced herself to meet his eyes. She was surprised to see uncertainty and doubt mirrored there, and could have flung her arms around his neck in gratitude.

Instead she rammed her hands into the back pockets of her jeans and gave him what she hoped was a smile. 'Hello, Oliver. Sorry I was so long.'

He searched her face, and his hand came out to cup her cheek. His thumb brushed lightly under her eye, and he frowned. 'Are you OK?'

She gave a strained little laugh. 'Of course. Why shouldn't I be?'

'You tell me. You just look tired and unhappy.'

She shook her head. 'Just tired. Last week was hard.'

He eyed her soberly. 'Are you telling me the truth? I don't want you to feel you're compromising your integrity by meeting me, Bron. I meant what I said. I want to be your friend. I would like to be very much more but, if I can't, fair enough. I have no intention of lying to you, now or ever, though. I want to wrap my arms around you and kiss you senseless, just to get that look of panic out of your eyes. But I won't. I want to get to know you. I don't expect it to be easy, but I'm going to give it my best shot. Now, before I give in to my baser instincts, shall we go for this walk?'

He grinned disarmingly, and she felt the tension go out of her on a ragged breath. Locking her car, she pocketed the keys and looked up at him.

'OK, let's go.'

They wandered through the wood, under the leafy canopy, and as if by some unwritten rule they kept their distance, taking exaggerated care to avoid any contact. When Oliver helped Bron over a stile, he immediately dropped her hand afterwards, ramming his hands back into his pockets as if he didn't trust them unless they were restrained.

They talked very little, and before long the tension was driving Bron mad. In the end she stopped in the middle of the track and waited.

He was so deep in thought that it was several seconds before Oliver realised he was on his own, and he turned and stared back at her for a long while before retracing his steps and coming to stand in front of her on the path.

'What's wrong?' he asked gently.

'Wrong?' Bron was horrified to hear a catch in her voice. 'I don't know. You seem so distant, so remote. There's so much tension between us. I can't cope with it.'

He gave a ragged sigh and ran his fingers through his already-tousled hair. 'There always was, Bron. That's the trouble. We can't ignore it, it isn't going to go away. We have to learn to get used to it, to make it into a part of our lives, to find a way of dealing with it.'

'"It"? What is this "it" you keep talking about?' Bron asked unhappily.

He tilted up her chin so that she was forced to meet his eyes, and the frustrated desire she saw there was softened by a melting tenderness that made her want to weep.

'Love. That's what we're talking about, Bron. Nothing more, nothing less. Just—love.'

She stared helplessly up into his eyes, drowning in the message in their vivid blue depths, and then with a low moan she sagged against his chest. 'It's so wrong,' she whispered brokenly, 'so wrong. . .'

His arms tightened about her, and she could hear the unsteady thud of his heart under her ear.

'It doesn't feel wrong, Bron. It feels right—very right. But we'll play it your way. I can be the perfect gentleman, if you're sure that's what you want.'

What she wanted and what she knew she ought to have were two entirely different animals, she recognised dully, but she pushed away from the warm haven of his arms with a wobbly smile and a sniff, and stuffed her hands back into her jeans pockets.

'Yes, that's what I want,' she lied shakily, and he gave a wry smile.

'If you say so, boss. Tell you what, let's go and get a cup of tea.'

They returned to the cars and Bron followed him out of the car park and back towards the town, turning off into a sought-after residential area at the top of the hill.

Funny place to get a cup of tea, Bron thought to herself, and then realised with a shock that he was turning into the drive of a big red-bricked Victorian house facing the park.

This must be his home, she thought, and curiosity

warred with caution as she turned carefully in behind him through the high gate-posts and pulled up with a scrunch on the gravel.

Curiosity won. She got out of the car and walked slowly towards him, trying to still the trembling of her heart. She wasn't entirely sure that she wanted to see the house where he lived with Clare, but she wasn't about to walk away now from a chance to get to know more about him.

'OK?' he asked with a lift to his eyebrows, and she nodded.

'I've got a few phone calls to make in the study. Would you like to put the kettle on?'

He showed her into the kitchen and then left her, stranded in a sea of childish finger-paintings held by a collection of magnetic numbers and letters on the front of the fridge, and a toy-box that seemed to be boiling over in the corner. On the wall above the breakfast-table was a photo of a little boy of about two, hair on end and a grubby smile on his face, eating an ice-cream with evident relish.

Bron felt frozen with shock, because the child looking back out at her could have been a younger Oliver—or an older Livvy. She stared at the photograph for an age, and then pulled herself together with an effort, clamping down hard on the urge to cry.

Make the tea, she told herself, and found the kettle almost by instinct. She filled it and put it on, and while it boiled she picked up the scattered toys and put them back in the toy-box.

'You don't have to do that,' Oliver said from behind her, and she laughed.

'Sorry. It's habit.'

'Habit?'

Oh, God, what had she said? She panicked into over-drive.

'I'm always clearing up after people. I'm a compulsive tidier-up. My father's banned me from his surgery, and Mum can't stand it when I get into the kitchen——'

You're babbling, she thought, and fell into silence.

'Don't be nervous, Bron, I'm not going to jump on you,' Oliver said quietly, and she sent up a quick, silent 'thank you' that he had misunderstood the reason for her sudden outburst.

He took over the making of the tea, and led her through into the conservatory at the back. The sun had gone off it by now and it was cool and green, a riot of lush foliage. Bron sank into the chair opposite Oliver and tried to ignore the wooden train on the floor.

He picked it up and chucked it on to the table.

'Toys everywhere in this house—you wouldn't think one small person could make such a mess.'

Oh, wouldn't I? she thought grimly, and sipped her tea in silence. How could he sit there and calmly talk about his son?

'What do you think of the house?'

She jumped at his sudden question, and gathered up her errant thoughts.

'It's lovely. I grew up in one very like it—I still live there, in fact, with my parents. Dad's a GP. Do you have a play-room?' she added. Now why do you want to know that? So you can torture yourself picturing him and his wife and son sprawled on the floor playing with the train-set? She gave a silent but disgusted sigh.

Oliver laughed shortly. 'There's a little sitting-room where we try and confine him when they come up for the weekend, but the little tyke treks things all over the house.'

Bron gave Oliver a startled look.

'What's the matter?'

She shrugged helplessly. 'Doesn't Clare live here with you?'

He shook his head. 'No. When I moved up here I suggested they come with me, but she's got all her friends in London, and she felt she'd be better there. She's got the house in Blackheath, and her nanny, and to be honest I don't think she wanted to leave her memories of Tom behind. It seemed cruel to press the point, but I made sure there was room for them here if she ever changed her mind, and they come most weekends.' His voice was wistful, and there was a haunting sadness in his eyes.

'Don't you miss them?'

He inspected the leaf on a geranium with unwarranted intensity, and then gave Bron a lop-sided grin. 'Of course, and the house only really comes alive when they're here. It can be very lonely. Come and have a look round.'

Stunned by his revelations, and amazed that Clare could possibly have stayed in London when she would have followed Oliver to the ends of the earth, Bron stood and trailed after him. He took her on a guided tour of the ground floor, and she found herself falling in love with the house. It was furnished warmly and comfortably, with no pretensions to grandeur but with a homely elegance completely at one with the style of the house. He explained that his parents had moved

from their family home into something more manage-
able, and he and his sister had custody of a lot of their
lovely old furniture.

'The dining-table, for instance—it looks Georgian,
because it is Georgian, but it's also got my initials
carved into the leg!'

'It shows that you didn't get an interior designer in,'
Bron said with a smile, and he shot her a worried look.

'Is it that bad?' he asked.

'Bad? Oh, Oliver, it's lovely! That's what I meant.
No stereotypical, designerish touches, just a warm and
comfortable home, the sort of place where you could
toast crumpets in front of the fire in the winter, lying
on the hearth-rug.' Bron didn't hear the wistfulness in
her voice, but Oliver did, and his face tensed with the
effort of controlling his emotions.

As they returned to the hall, he eyed the stairs with
misgivings.

'I don't think I trust myself to show you the rest,' he
said softly and, tucking his hand through her arm, he
led her back to the conservatory. 'More tea?'

She shook her head. 'I don't think so, Oliver. I really
ought to be going. It's been—nice.'

He gave a long, ragged sigh, and looked at her with
tortured eyes, all pretence abandoned.

'It's been hell, Bron—sheer, unmitigated bloody
hell! But it beats the pants off the past two years,
wondering where you were, how you were, why you
hadn't answered the letters I'd sent to the hospital—
God, I missed you. If you had any idea——'

He turned away abruptly, his shoulders rigid, his
head bowed, and Bron fought the urge to fling her
arms around him and hold him close to her breast, to

smooth back his hair and kiss away the pain. Because of course she understood, every last moment of agony, and then some.

'Oliver, I must go——'

He straightened, and turned back to her, his eyes shuttered. 'Sorry, Bron. I didn't mean to break the rules. And it was good to spend time with you. Perhaps if we do it often enough we'll get used to it.'

He led her to the front door, and then paused. For a long, breathless moment he stared down into her eyes, and then his gaze fell slowly to take in her lips, then down over the unsteady rise and fall of her breasts, down over her slender hips and legs clad in jeans that now seemed provocatively tight, and then back up, burning a trail over her body, until their eyes clashed and held.

Her lips parted on a shaky breath, and her tongue eased out to moisten them. Oliver closed his eyes with a groan.

'For God's sake, Bron, get out of here,' he said in a harsh whisper, and she opened the door with shaking hands, slamming it behind her and running over the gravel to her car.

With trembling fingers, she fitted the key into the ignition and started the car, turning round in the drive and heading out towards the road. As she reached the gate-posts, she glanced back in the rear-view mirror and saw Oliver standing in the doorway, watching her intently. Even from here she could feel the heat in his eyes.

As she pulled out on to the road, the first scalding tears spilled over her lashes and tracked down her flushed cheeks, falling unheeded on to her lap.

'Oh, Clare, I'm sorry,' she whispered, and dashed the tears away. She knew she was wrong to feel this way about another woman's husband, but, try as she might, she couldn't help herself. The best she could hope for was to be able to disguise her feelings—and hope she did it better than Oliver, she thought, and her heart ached for the wrenching sadness in his eyes, and the desperate yearning she had seen just before he'd closed them and told her to go.

Well, that's that, she thought sadly; there was no way they could ever share a simple friendship. They would just have to bury their feelings during working hours, and avoid each other like the plague, because of one thing she was absolutely sure. If Oliver had been within a hair's breadth of giving in, she had been even closer to surrender.

She managed to avoid him during the following week, although she wasn't sure who was doing the avoiding hardest. His surgical registrar became a frequent visitor to A and E, and it reached the point where even Jim Harris remarked on Oliver's absence.

'Have you two fallen out?' he asked with a laugh, and Bron managed a light-hearted reply before running away gratefully in answer to her bleep.

On Friday Jim and Jesus Marumba cornered her and told her to come over to the pub with them. She declined with difficulty, and made her way instead to the staff dining-room, certain that Oliver would be firmly ensconced in the pub.

She had just sat down with her tray when a shadow fell across her plate.

'Mind if I join you?'

She closed her eyes and counted to ten. 'Not at all, but do you think it's wise?'

'Damned if I know any more,' Oliver muttered, easing himself down on to the chair opposite. 'One thing's for sure, avoiding you doesn't seem to get you out of my mind. Perhaps we ought to try for over-exposure, and bore each other to bits.'

Bron laughed. 'Oh, Oliver. You are an idiot. I'm only here because I thought you'd be in the pub.'

He chuckled. 'Ditto. Oh, well, the best-laid plans and all that. Eat up, we'll go over and join them for a swift half before battle recommences.'

By the time they arrived at the pub, Mick O'Shea and Steve Barnes were there as well, and Bron raised an eyebrow. 'Who's in A and E?'

'You,' Jim mumbled through a mouthful of prawn salad, and looked pointedly from Bron to Oliver and back. 'You two got something going?'

'Don't be absurd!' Bron joked, and Jim opened his mouth to comment.

'Mind your own damn business, Jim,' Oliver growled, and Jim subsided with a speculative twinkle.

'Say no more,' he murmured, and stabbed a prawn. 'Soul of discretion, me. Not a word out of place.'

'Wrap it!' Oliver warned in an undertone, and Jim raised an eyebrow, but obligingly fell silent.

Jesus looked from one to the other and then concentrated on drawing patterns with a wet finger on the table-top.

'Coming to the League of Friends summer fair tomorrow, Bron?' he asked, and Bron snatched gratefully at the uncontroversial red herring.

'Maybe. What time is it?'

'Starts at two. We'll all be there, of course, in the stocks. Ten pence a throw with wet sponges.'

She grinned. 'Sounds too good to miss. Iced water, is it?'

Oliver choked. 'I never realised you were sadistic—or is this getting your own back for some imagined slight?'

Fortunately her bleep went and rescued her yet again. She wondered how she would have survived without it.

She sounded her mother out that night about the fair, hoping that she would be able to have Livvy, but her mother had a better idea.

'Let David look after her, and let's go together. I'd like to get a look at this Oliver of yours—maybe even chuck a sponge at him. God knows, he deserves it.'

'Mum, I shan't tell you who he is if you make threats like that!'

Her mother laughed gently and squeezed her daughter's shoulders. 'You can trust me, darling, but I would like to catch a glimpse of the man who fathered my grandchild—however inadvertently.'

So they went together, and left Livvy going with her indulgent grandfather to feed the ducks. They found the stocks by the howls and shrieks, and had to join a queue composed mainly of nurses lining up for a rare opportunity to have a go at the consultants.

When Bron caught sight of Oliver, it nearly took her breath away. He was sitting, legs outstretched and trapped by the wooden stocks, wearing just a pair of brief swimming-trunks and a huge smile, ducking madly and hiding his head behind his arms. His body was tanned and fit-looking, and the sun glinted in the water coursing down through the wet tangle of curls on his chest.

Jesus, beside him, was just as wet, just as heart-stoppingly handsome and just as cheerful about his fate.

Bron pointed them out to her mother, and she nodded and squeezed Bron's hand in silent sympathy. 'I can see why you fell for him,' she murmured in an undertone, and Bron laughed.

'So can everyone else at the moment. Just wait till it's my go!'

When it was Bron's turn, she picked up a sopping sponge, called to Oliver, to get his attention, and lobbed the sponge straight at his head.

He took it full in the face, and came up laughing, throwing it back to land with a wet plop on the front of Bron's T-shirt.

'Hey, not fair!' she yelled, and Mick O'Shea appeared behind Oliver.

'You want me to hold him still, Bron?'

'Thank you, Mick. Nice and steady. . .'

She grabbed a loaded sponge, took careful aim, and missed, soaking Mick.

Oliver let down his guard and roared with laughter, but it was a mistake. Both Bronwen and her mother let fly with deadly accuracy.

'Oh, good shot!' Jesus crowed, and then they turned their attention to him.

After three sponges each, Bron and her mother made their way to the tea-tent, still laughing.

'Poor Oliver,' Bron said weakly, and Elizabeth grinned.

'He owed me that. It gave me great satisfaction.'

Bron sobered. 'Oh, Mum. It wasn't his fault. None of it was his fault. He isn't a philanderer, I'd stake my life on it. If he felt the way I felt, he couldn't help himself.'

Her mother eyed her seriously. 'You never did tell me what happened last weekend.'

Bron sighed. 'Nothing—by a minor miracle. We ruled out the possibility of friendship, though!'

'Oh, lord, Bron. Don't let him hurt you again.'

'His very existence hurts me, Mum. To know him is to be hurt by him—and none of it is his fault.'

They finished their tea soberly, and then made their way over to the craft stalls.

Elizabeth held up a little dress with a smocked bodice and puff-sleeves. 'Bron, look! Isn't this a darling little dress? Let's get it for Livvy.'

'Who's Livvy?' murmured a deep voice from over her shoulder, and Bron started and dropped her purse.

'Here, let me help.' Oliver crouched down beside her on the grass and picked up scattered coins, old till-receipts and theatre tickets.

As he handed the things back to her, their eyes locked, crouched down among the legs and swinging skirts, with Bron's awareness of him like a living thing between them, binding them with its tentacles. She could hardly breathe, with his hard thigh pressed against her own, the coarse hairs chafing against her skin where her skirt had ridden up above her knees. He had pulled on a T-shirt, but his legs were still bare, and she could see the muscles rippling under the skin as he moved.

'Who's Livvy?' he repeated, and sanity returned like a bucketful of cold water.

'She's—a friend's child,' Bron said with an element of truth, and straightened awkwardly to her feet, tugging her skirt into line and praying for a miracle.

It came in the form of Jesus, stumbing through the crowd with his hand clapped over his eye, searching the throng with the other eye for any sign of his friend.

'Oliver! Help me, could you? Some damn fool chucked a handful of mud at me and got me a bull's-eye. I think it could do with a good swill.'

'Come on, let's migrate to A and E. Coming, Bron?'

'Um—yes, OK. Hang on.' She turned to her mother. 'Come with us—you can meet the team. You might as well.'

The lady manning the craft stall took the money for the little dress, and then Bron and Elizabeth followed Jesus and Oliver through the crowd towards A and E.

'What did you tell him?' Elizabeth asked in an undertone.

'That she's a friend's child. I suppose technically it might be true. Oh, God, it's getting so complicated!'

Steve Barnes was already busy with a patient, so Bron pulled on her white coat, ushered Jesus into one of the treatment-rooms, and proceeded to deal with the mud.

'What an idiot!' she said crossly. 'You could have been badly hurt!'

Jesus gave a snort of laughter. 'Excuse me, lady, from this side it feels like I already am!'

'Rubbish! Now for heaven's sake lie still before I poke your eye out. Honestly. . .doctors!' she muttered, and removed the last trace of grit with a damp swab. 'There, how's that?'

Jesus blinked experimentally. 'Better, I think. You didn't make too much of a hash of that, considering you're a mere woman,' he teased gently, and swung his bare legs over the edge of the couch.

'Thanks, I think,' Bron said drily, and turned to her mother. 'Mum, I want you to meet Jesus Marumba, one of our consultant physicians, and Oliver Henderson——'

'Oh, Oliver and I have introduced ourselves while you've been fiddling about with that eye. And you're Jesus. I've been hearing a lot about you all, so it's nice to meet you in person.'

'How about a cup of coffee?' Bron suggested.

'What a wonderful idea,' said a warm, low voice from behind her.

'Oh, girls! Perfect timing. Bron, meet Jesus's wife, Lucy. Lucy, this is Bronwen Jones, our new A and E registrar.'

Bron turned towards the voice, and froze.

There were two women—one the tall, elegant and unmistakably pregnant Lucy Marumba, and, beside her, her fair skin and platinum-blonde hair set off to perfection by the glowing ebony of Lucy's dark tones, was a fragile beauty with soft green eyes and a warm, generous smile.

Her heart in her throat, Bron murmured a greeting to Lucy. Behind her, she could hear Oliver introducing Lucy to her mother, but her attention was all on the slender young woman in front of her.

She would have known her anywhere—not because she recognised her, but because of the grubby, exhausted little boy who had fallen asleep in her arms, his absurdly long lashes dark crescents against his pale cheeks.

'Hello, Clare,' she said quietly.

CHAPTER FIVE

AFTERWARDS Bron wasn't sure how she got through the next few minutes.

Oliver stepped forward and took the sleeping child from Clare's arms with a tender smile that wrenched at her heart, and turned to her. 'Bron, I'd like you to meet my——'

'We've introduced ourselves,' Bron said quickly, and turned to the child as the least controversial of the available options. 'And this is Tom. He's— gorgeous. . .'

Her voice was unconsciously wistful, and her mother shot her a worried look.

Clare laughed. 'I don't know about gorgeous—he's heavy! And I could murder a coffee if there is any. It's thirsty work dragging that small urchin around!'

While Bronwen was still deciding how to deal with her tangled emotions, she heard her mother's voice quietly at her elbow.

'If you wouldn't mind, Bron, I could do with going home now and skipping coffee.'

'Don't worry,' Jesus put in, 'we know where the coffee is. You go on if you have to. See you on Monday.'

As they reached the car, Bron chucked her keys to her mother.

'You drive, could you?' she said tightly. 'I don't think I'd be safe.'

83

She sat motionless, staring blindly out of the windscreen all the way home, and willing herself not to fly apart inside. Every time her eyes closed, she conjured up a vision of Oliver standing with Tom cradled in his arms, and the pain grew until she was sure that the hard knot in her chest must be visible.

She refused to discuss it with her mother, and when they got in she excused herself and took Livvy upstairs to bath her.

Watching the little imp playing in the bath reminded her so forcibly of Tom and Oliver that the threatening tears spilt over her lashes and tracked slowly down her cheeks; only Livvy's exuberant splashing saved her from detection when her mother came in a little while later to bring her a drink.

'Gin and tonic,' she said economically, and thrust it into Bron's hand. 'Frankly, you look as if you need it. Get that child to bed and let's talk.'

'I don't want to talk. There's nothing to say.'

'Rubbish. There's everything to say. Your father's going out on a call. I'll see you in the drawing-room in half an hour.'

It was nearly three quarters of an hour before Bron was able to screw up enough courage to face her mother. When she entered the drawing-room, the blinds were closed against the slanting rays of the evening sun, and the room was cool and dim. Helping herself to another drink, Bron found a dark corner and sank miserably into a chair.

'What did you want to say?' she asked wearily.

Her mother fiddled with the safety-chain on her watch, and then sighed heavily. What she was going to say wasn't easy, but had to be said.

'Bron, he still loves her. And he loves you too. That much was as plain as a pikestaff from the way he was looking at you, but I think you want to remember that there are different kinds of love.'

Bron swallowed. 'Such as?'

'Such as the tender, enduring but largely passionless love he obviously feels for Clare and Tom, and the blind, white-hot desire he feels for you.'

Bron's hand shook and she slopped her drink all over her skirt. Brushing it off with trembling fingers, she swallowed hard at the lump in her throat. 'Is it so very obvious?'

'Only to me. It reminds me of the way your father looked at me when we were your age. And it shows in your eyes when you look at him.'

Bron shook her head. 'Mum, it isn't just physical——'

'I never said it was, Bron,' her mother returned quietly. 'I simply said it was white-hot. And don't for a moment imagine that you are going to be able to control it. It'll burn you out before you do. Believe me, I know. You'll feel him enter a room behind you, you'll know he's going to call you a second before the phone rings, and every time you hear his name your heart will leap in your chest. Trust me, Bron. I've been there.'

'Is there a cure?' Bron asked wistfully.

Her mother smiled tenderly. 'Thirty-two years has shown a definite decline in the severity of the symptoms, but they're still clearly recognisable.' Her smile faded. 'Oh, Bron, I wish I could help you.'

Her daughter closed her eyes and silent tears

squeezed between her lids and splashed on to her hands. 'So do I, Mum—so do I.'

It was the longest weekend of her life. She walked miles through the woods where she had walked with Oliver, and retraced their steps, reliving every word, every gesture.

She longed for Monday, to put an end to the time she had on her hands, and yet she dreaded going back to the hospital and seeing Oliver again. She needn't have worried. He had flu and was off for the first three days, and then spent Thursday on his elective list.

On Thursday night she was on call, and spent the evening sewing up drunks and attending to the general run of summer-evening trivia like tennis elbows and golf backs.

One young man had serious burns on his hands from slipping and falling into a barbecue pit, and she sent him home after treating the injury.

She was just heading for the sanctuary of her little room when a woman was admitted with a heavy pv bleed. She turned and retraced her footsteps.

'Seen her GP?' she asked the nurse, and received a shrug in reply.

'Not this time. The GP said he wasn't prepared to come out to visit a woman just because she had a heavy period. He told her to go to bed and see him at the surgery in the morning.'

Bron rolled her eyes and entered the cubicle. The woman, a pretty brunette in her late thirties, was looking very pale and weak.

'Hello, my love. What's the problem?'

Gently, sympathetically, Bron coaxed a history of

long, painful and heavy periods, becoming steadily worse over the past year. While she was talking, Bron watched her bloodless lips and was horrified at the pallor. Whatever the reason, the patient was obviously grossly anaemic.

'I think we need to get blood for HB and cross-matching, just to be on the safe side,' she said to the nurse who appeared again at her elbow.

'Now how did I know you were going to say that, Dr Jones?' the nurse said with a grin. Bron saw that she already had the syringe in her hand.

With an answering smile, she peeled back the blanket and barely controlled a gasp of dismay. The hand-towel pressed between the woman's thighs was soaked with blood and, when Bron removed it, she could see the blood welling with each slight movement her patient made.

She removed the towel and placed a sanitary pad in its place, checking her watch for the time, and then replaced the blanket.

'I'm just going to get one of the gynae doctors down to look at you, Mrs Andrews,' Bron explained, and made her way to the sister's office.

'Can you get me the gynae SHO on take, please?' she asked the switchboard, and within minutes a harassed young man appeared.

'This better be urgent, Dr Jones,' he mumbled. 'I've got three mums in labour, and two more on their way in.'

'Heavy pv bleed,' she explained, and he groaned.

'You got me down here just because some silly cow's having a heavy period?' he muttered under his breath.

It was not meant for her ears, but nevertheless Bron

ground her teeth together and counted to ten, then she let him have it.

'Her blood pressure is ninety over fifty. She appears to be grossly anaemic, and has had a history of increasingly severe bleeding over the past year. Her uterus is very enlarged, and I would imagine she's got galloping fibroids. Any minute now she's going to bleed to death. Now get off your goddamn arrogant little high horse and attend to your patient before you make any more unfounded and sexist remarks!'

She marched him up the corridor and twitched the curtain aside, gentling her manner as she approached the bed. 'Mrs Andrews, this is Dr Ward. He's just going to have a look at you, OK?'

The young man glowered at Bron, managed a barely civil 'hello' to Mrs Andrews, and hooked off the blanket without finesse.

'OK, when did you last change this pad?' he asked in a bored voice. He was all but tapping his foot.

'Seven minutes ago,' Bron replied quietly, and he snapped to attention.

'Right, let's have some blood off to the lab for cross-matching and haemoglobin levels——'

'Done,' Bron replied wearily, 'and we've ordered four units to be sent to Theatre. Your registrar is on the way in, and Theatre's been alerted. She's signed the consent form. Perhaps you could find time to talk to her husband—he's in the waiting-room.'

She could hardly be bothered to keep the sarcasm out of her voice. Chastened, the young SHO left the cubicle and Bron covered Mrs Andrews up again.

'Don't worry, my love. They'll sort you out soon.'

The porter arrived to take her to Theatre, and Dr Ward departed, mumbling an apology.

Suppressing a grin, Bron headed for the staff-room and a much-needed cup of coffee before turning in.

'Well said, Dr Jones,' a disembodied voice pronounced from the depths of the room.

Bron's heart went into overdrive. Controlling the urge to run, she stayed to fight and flipped the light-switch. 'Hello, Oliver. What brings you down here?'

He grinned. 'A better standard of coffee. What a pompous little bastard!'

She chuckled. 'Yes, I enjoyed telling him so. I really think men ought to be compulsorily tested for misogynous tendencies before they're allowed into medicine—especially areas like obs and gynae!'

'We'd all fail,' Oliver said lazily, and added, 'How about a cup of coffee, squaw?'

There was a curled-up sandwich lying on the table next to the coffee. She threw it at him.

'Missed!'

'Just a warning. There's the other half,' she threatened laughingly, and then her breath caught in her throat as she turned to look at him. He was dressed in theatre greens, the fabric pulled taut across his thighs as he lay sprawled in the chair, and he looked weary and infinitely desirable.

Bron handed him a coffee, and retreated with hers to the other side of the room. 'Are you on call?'

He nodded. 'I was hoping to have a lazy night, but I think it's going to be one of those when it's just not worth going home.'

'Come and crash down here,' she suggested, and he raised an eyebrow.

'With or without you?'

She laughed, a little breathlessly. 'Without, almost guaranteed. It's going to be one of those nights for me too, I'm sure. If so, you might as well have the room. Last week I lay down for twenty minutes, twice.'

He gave a slow, wicked smile. 'I shall look forward to those minutes,' he teased. 'I'll see you later.'

He unfolded himself from the chair and left, whistling softly under his breath. Bron wondered what on earth she was thinking about, inviting him to use her room?

Poking sleeping tigers again, she thought, and groaned. One day she'd learn to keep her mouth shut.

The next hour was quiet, and she managed to catch a little sleep before the staff nurse tapped on her door.

'RTA warning, Bron. ETA five minutes. Seven casualties, some slight, some severe. One chap with head injuries, and another the fire crew are still cutting out of his vehicle.'

Bron groaned, dragged on her white coat and buttoned it up over her slip, running a comb through her hair on the way to the door.

'Have you notified Neurology?'

The nurse nodded. 'Yes, and Mr Henderson's coming down. I gather there are several internal injuries. The orthopaedic reg. is already here, and the radiographer's ready. I've contacted the lab for blood, and they're on stand-by to bring in further supplies if necessary.'

Oliver arrived at her elbow and winked encouragingly.

'Grab a coffee before we start?' he suggested, and she nodded, wondering with a small and detached part of her mind how he could even bear to look at her. She was sure her eyes were red-rimmed and bloodshot, and she felt about as inspiring as the curled-up sandwich she had lobbed at him earlier.

'Chin up, Bron. Soon be over. Right, what details have we got so far?'

She outlined briefly what the nurse had been able to tell her as they drank their coffee, and then the ambulances arrived and the time for speculation was over.

'Hi-ho, hi-ho,' Oliver said cheerfully, and went to find the patients with internal injuries.

The man with head wounds was in a critical condition, and Bron dealt with him first, quickly assessing the extent of his injuries. The neurology SR, Simon Baines, arrived as she was finishing her examination, and she shook her head.

'Fractured base of skull, I think. He's leaking CSF from his nose and his left ear. I'm getting no response to anything. His pupils are uneven and unreactive, no response to stimulus, no reflexes. We're having to ventilate him artificially now, although he was breathing under his own steam when he arrived. There's a nasty compression over his left ear, as well, and I think he may have spinal injuries. His lumbar spine feels sort of lumpy.'

The registrar nodded grimly, and slid his hand carefully under the man's waist, palm up. He nodded again. 'Sheered clean through L3.' He threaded his fingers carefully through the man's hair and felt his skull, then sighed. 'Craked like an egg, isn't it? We'll run a brainstem test, but I don't think we'll find a glimmer. Damn! Any ID on him?'

'Yes, so I understand. His name's Donald Armstrong. His wife was in the car with him. She's got lower-limb injuries, from what I gather, but nothing drastic. There's a policeman outside with the details.'

'Go and see to the wife while I talk to the policeman, then I'll come and have a word with her.'

Bron left the cubicle and found the man's wife, who, despite the extent of her own injuries, was wild with worry for her husband.

She clutched Bron's hand and hung on to it for dear life. 'How's Don?' she asked desperately, and Bron took a deep breath. Should she lie? Be economical with the truth, she decided, and let her breath out in a rush.

'The neurologist is with him now. He seems to have a fractured skull, and spinal injuries. They're still assessing the extent of the damage. Now, can I have a look at you?'

'Can I see him?'

'Not at the moment. Let me take a look at your legs, Mrs Armstrong.' Bron lifted the blanket away from the cage over her patient's legs, and winced inwardly. Her gentle but thorough fingers reduced the woman to stoical silence for a few moments, and then Bron replaced the covers. 'You'll need some X-rays and, I think, an operation to line up the bones correctly in your left leg. Now, how about the rest of you? Any pain anywhere else?' she asked as she ran her hands carefully over the other limbs and listened to her chest and abdomen.

Mrs Armstrong shook her head numbly, and Bron started filling in the requst for the X-rays. 'There, that should do it. You'll need to sign a consent form for your operation, and for your husband. I'll go and find the neurologist and see if he can have a word——'

'Is he going to die?'

Bron forced herself to meet the woman's eyes. 'I don't know. Maybe. He's very severely injured. I hope I'm wrong, but the signs aren't good. I'll get the doctor——'

'If he dies—he always carries a donor card. I know he'd want——' She bit her lip and turned her head away.

'Thank you,' Bron said quietly. 'If it comes to that, we'll bear his wishes in mind. Hopefully it won't.' She slipped out to find Simon Baines. They met in the corridor, and Bron led him out of earshot.

'Any change?'

'Not a sausage. I think he's had it. How's the Mrs?'

Bron gave a short, mirthless laugh. 'Says he always carried a donor card. I think she's running on auto-pilot at the moment. I don't think it's hit her yet.'

Simon shot her a surprised look. 'Did you tell her?'

'She asked me. I couldn't lie. She's not stupid, Simon, she saw him. I told her maybe.'

'Mmm. Well, I think it's a bit more than maybe, but we'll leave it at that until she's a bit stronger. I've rung the chief; he's coming in and we're going to run the brain-stem test. I'll tell Mrs Armstrong the result when we have it. Until then, I suppose I'd better give an edited version of the truth first-hand. How bad is she?'

'Fractured right tibia, multiple fracture of left tibia and fibula, nasty mess around the knee-joint—I think she's going to be lucky not to lose it.'

Simon shook his head and his mouth tightened to a

grim line. 'Life's a bitch, and then you die,' he muttered, and entered the cubicle with a gentle smile. 'Mrs
Armstrong? My name's Simon Baines. I've just been
looking after your husband.'

Bron left them together, and arranged for a nurse to
stay with Mrs Armstrong while she waited for her
X-rays; then she found the orthopaedic reg. and asked
him to take a look at her. While she was sitting at the
desk in the office, writing up notes, Oliver came in and
picked up the phone. He looked weary and kind, and
Bron was enormously glad to see him. She had to fight
the urge to snuggle into his arms and lay her head on
his chest and go to sleep, and concentrated on filling in
forms and catching up with paperwork on the
Armstrongs.

'Digging my registrar out of bed,' he said, hitching
one hip up on to the edge of the desk, and grinning
wryly. 'Don't see why we should have all the fun to
ourselves. How are you doing?'

She answered his smile with difficulty. 'OK. It's a
nasty one.'

He nodded. 'Not fair. I was looking forward to
curling up in your bed—oh, hello, Mike.' He laughed
and grinned again, and the years fell away from him.
'No, not yours. Look, we've got a bit of a panic on
down here. Could you come in? I've got a couple of
urgent cases, so I'll need you in the other theatre.
Good man.'

He replaced the receiver, and ruffled Bron's hair as
he straightened and moved towards the door. 'I'm
going up to Theatre—there's a woman with multiple
internal injuries, and a man with a ruptured spleen.
It'll probably take hours! I'll see you for breakfast.'

Bron's mouth lifted in a slight smile, and she nodded. 'It's a deal.' She watched him go, and then lifted herself wearily out of the chair and followed him. She could still feel the touch of his hand, warm against her hair, and it went with her—a tender gesture of comfort in the grim hours that followed.

She dealt with the other casualties, mopping up, stitching, filling in forms and handing out head-injury cards, treating shock, and generally restoring order from chaos until the last victim was brought in, remarkably cheerful considering the long and painful struggle to free him from the wreckage of his car.

Fortunately he was only suffering from cuts and bruises, with a nasty sprain to his right ankle and a real gem of a black eye. Bron tidied him up, admitted him for observation, and tumbled into bed, asleep almost before her head hit the pillow.

In her dreams she felt the bed dip beside her, and a pair of warm, strong arms wrapped themselves around her. She snuggled her head against a solid chest and sighed with contentment.

She was woken by a bleep, and struggled to sit up, but there seemed to be something heavy over her legs, and a band tightened around her chest as she tried to move.

'It's mine,' a voice mumbled in her ear, and she dragged herself back to consciousness as Oliver sat up and swung his legs over the edge of the bed. He fumbled for the light and then picked up the phone, calling in. 'Henderson,' he said gruffly, and Bron watched as he dialled ITU.

His eyes were red-rimmed, his face grey with exhaustion, and he desperately need a shave, but Bron thought she had never seen anything more welcome. As he spoke, he ran a hand through his sleep-tousled hair, and then he stilled and closed his eyes. The lines etched deeply into his face, and he pressed his lips together and swallowed hard. 'OK, thanks. I'll be down in a few minutes.'

He replaced the receiver.

'Bad news?' she asked quietly, and he let out his breath on a harsh sigh and nodded.

'The woman with internal injuries. I thought we might lose her, but—oh, damn!'

Bron opened her arms to him, and he leaned over and rested his head against her shoulder. 'I thought I dreamt you,' she said after a long moment, and he shook his head slightly.

'No, what there is of me is real, bloodshot eyes and all. God, you feel good, Bron—warm and soft and infinitely inviting.'

He lifted his head and looked down at her, and as she met his eyes she knew that he was going to kiss her, knew the inevitability of it and rejoiced in it. As his lips came down, hers parted on a sigh of welcome, and they clung together, drowning in a whirling maelstrom of savage tenderness so strong that Bron thought she would die.

Then he eased away, his eyes dark with passion, and brushed his lips lightly across her forehead before pulling on his shoes and rising to his feet. 'I have to go,' he murmured huskily. 'I'll see you in the pub for lunch if not before. Bron, I——' He broke off, and then passed his hand over his face in a gesture of weary resignation. 'I'll see you later.'

He closed the door behind him with a soft click, and

Bron turned out the light and snuggled down into the bed again, her mind in turmoil. There were faint traces of his cologne lingering on the pillow, and mixed with it a more personal scent that curled around her senses and tangled in her insides.

'Now what?' she asked herself, and, coming up with no acceptable answer, she turned her face into the pillow and contented herself with the memory of that all-too-brief kiss. . ., a kiss that had left a yearning, unsettling ache deep inside her—an ache that time had failed to erase.

CHAPTER SIX

IT SEEMED to have been a busy night all round. When Bron dug herself out of bed at seven for a quick wash, she had had precisely two hours' sleep in three short stretches, and her bleary eyes stared blankly back at her from the mirror. She poked her tongue out half-heartedly at herself, dragged a comb through the tangled wreckage of her hair, and dabbed a touch of pink lipstick on to add a little colour to her wan face. Then she headed for the staff dining-room to eat a huge breakfast, having had neither the time nor the energy to eat during the night.

She was not alone. The gynae SHO, looking suitably chastened, grinned nervously at her in the queue.

'You were right about Mrs Andrews,' he said apologetically. 'She had massive fibroids, apparently. Look, I'm sorry about——'

'Good,' Bron cut in, 'I should hope so. Your remarks last night stank. I think you ought to have a long, hard look at your motives and prejudices before you settle on an all-female speciality.' She turned away and bumped into Oliver, who was grinning broadly. 'Oh, hello.'

'Hello yourself. Are you hell-bent on destroying his confidence?' he asked mildly as the young man grabbed his breakfast and fled.

'Yes,' she retorted crossly, 'if that's all it takes. He's got no business in medicine, never mind gynae, with that attitude.' She helped herself to bacon, eggs, tomatoes and toast.

Oliver shook his head and tutted at her. 'Poor boy. He was probably just panic-stricken. He had Jesus peering over his shoulder most of the night.'

Bron frowned. 'Jesus?'

Oliver nodded and loaded his plate. 'Lucy had the baby at about five this morning—while we were curled up together pushing up zeds,' he murmured, eyes twinkling.

Bron ignored the innuendo. 'What is it?'

'Huge and vigorous, I gather! A girl—mother and baby doing well——'

'Which is more than can be said for the father,' a deep voice muttered behind them.

'Jesus! Congratulations!' Bron flung her arms around him and gave him a huge hug. 'How's Lucy?'

His heart-stopping smile split his face, and he gave an exultant laugh. 'Wonderful. Amazing. It's going to be an only child, though. No way am I letting Lucy go through that again!'

'Rubbish,' Bron admonished. 'Piece of cake. You soon forget the pain, and it's the most fantastic experience——'

'Anyone would think you'd done it,' Oliver said quietly, and she looked quickly away, her heart racing and a guilty flush running up her cheeks. She gave a— hopefully—light-hearted chuckle.

'All my friends are at the baby stage at the moment—it's all I hear morning, noon and night. Believe me, Lucy will soon be talking about the next one.'

Jesus shook his head. 'She'll have to do it without

my help, then, because I'm damned if I can cope with it!'

Oliver made a wisecrack about immaculate conception, and Jesus grinned wickedly.

'I don't intend to be virtuous—just careful!' he said with a laugh.

They paid for their food and moved across to sit by the window. The dew was sparkling on the grass, and the sun's warming rays gilded the wet flagstones of the path. It was a wonderful morning, a golden morning just like the one fifteen months ago when Bron had woken and looked down into the face of her brand-new daughter. She felt a familiar clutch of sadness that Oliver hadn't been there to share the long and lonely night with her, had missed the glorious moment of Livvy's birth and the joys and sleepless nights of the next few months.

Instead it had been her mother there by her side, holding her hand and encouraging her, admiring the baby, hugging Bron and making the few necessary phone calls; her mother who had seen her through the sleepless nights; her father who had seen Livvy sit up for the first time, watched her first stumbling steps, supported Bron emotionally and financially until she was ready to face the world again.

She was eternally grateful to them for their love and non-judgemental support, but she wished it had been Oliver. Tears glistened on her lashes, and she brushed them angrily aside.

Oliver frowned, and Jesus tipped up her chin and stared searchingly into her eyes. She sniffed inelegantly and gave them a wobbly smile. 'New babies always do this to me,' she explained feebly, and Oliver laughed.

'Sometimes I think I'll never understand women,' he said wryly, and turned his attention to his breakfast, engaging Jesus in conversation.

Although he responded, Jesus didn't look away from her face, searching it with the meticulous thoroughness of the good physician. Then he gave her a slight, understanding smile, and attacked his breakfast. 'Missed supper,' he said with a mouthful of bacon and egg, and Bron laughed shakily and poked the food on her plate with the tines of her fork.

Her appetite had deserted her, and she was relieved when her bleep went and she could legitimately leave it and return to the relative tranquillity of A and E.

Had Jesus guessed? She supposed it was inevitable that it would get out in the end, if only because one day someone would be bound to see her with Livvy in the town. She couldn't keep it a secret forever, and she didn't know how she would deal with it when it did leak out, but she knew one thing—she wasn't ready to deal with it yet.

A and E was its usual chaotic self by the time she got back, and she took a deep breath and dived in. A scalded hand from the kettle, a broken arm from a tumble down the stairs—late, apparently as usual, for school—and a finger trapped in the car-door in the haste to get to work, were the first priority, and Bron dealt with them automatically, dishing out smiles and reassurances as if they were aspirin as she worked.

Kathleen Hennessy came on at nine, and, with the spate of early-morning traumas out of the way, there was a slight lull. Bron slumped into a chair and gratefully took the coffee Kathleen handed her. There were doughnuts, too, courtsey of someone's birthday, and Bron nibbled half-heartedly at one.

'Why don't you go to bed?' Kathleen asked. 'You look like hell.'

'Thanks,' Bron muttered, 'that's really cheered me up no end!'

'I mean it,' the sister continued. 'It's quiet for once— go and get forty winks, and I'll get you if you're needed. Jim's here now, and Steve and Mick are about somewhere. Go on.'

Reluctantly Bron followed Kathleen's advice and went and lay down on top of the bed, falling asleep in seconds. The night had taken its toll, and she slept without stirring for two hours. Then hunger drove her out of bed, and she freshened up and went back to join the fray.

'You look better,' Kathleen said approvingly, and handed her some notes. 'You're just in time. We've got a Mr Harding in the trauma unit with chest and right-arm pain. It apparently came on suddenly in the middle of a board meeting, and he says the pain's very severe. He's got no previous history, and he looks fit enough—he's forty-eight.'

Bron nodded her thanks and went into the treatment cubicle. Jennifer, one of the duty nurses, was setting up the heart monitor.

'Hello, Mr Harding,' she said with a smile, and watched him as he turned his head slowly towards her. His face was taut with pain, and his breathing was laboured. She went through his symptoms with him and kept a weather-eye on the monitor, analysing the pattern, then she smiled again. 'I'll get the medical registrar to come and have a look at you, and we'll go from there.'

'It's a heart attack, isn't it?' he asked calmly, and Bron nodded.

'Yes, I think so. Just rest, Mr Harding, and try and relax. We'll soon have you comfortable.'

She went into the sister's office and picked up the phone. 'Medical reg. on take, please,' she said, and the phone was taken out of her hand.

'Cancel that, it's under control,' Jesus said, and turned to Bron. 'OK, what's the problem?'

'Forty-eight-year-old man with chest and right-arm pain. From the trace I'd say he's had an anterior MI.'

'And what do you think we should do?'

'I was about to give some pain relief and start him on streptokinase.'

'Why?'

'Because it reduces the incidence of death by half if given in the first four hours, and he's only had the pain for about an hour at the outside, so there's a good chance it'll work.'

'Why not tPA?'

Bron's eyes widened. 'It costs ten times as much!'

'Should that be a consideration?'

'Yes, of course—when the results are the same. It means ten times as many people can be treated——'

Jesus smiled. 'Precisely my sentiments. Let's go and take a look.'

Half an hour later, the patient, now admitted, was out of pain, the IV line was in and the streptokinase drip was running, and Bron and Jesus were back in the staff-room, sipping coffee.

'How come you were down here?' Bron asked.

'Oh, this and that.' Jesus laughed slightly, and looked up to meet her eyes. 'Actually, I was looking for you.' He paused, as if considering his words carefully. 'I take it no one else knows?'

'Knows what?' Bron tried to make her voice sound casual, and failed dismally.

'Bron, please trust me. It was obvious you were much more upset than Lucy's baby warranted. Why?' he prodded gently. 'Have you got a child?'

Blindly Bron nodded. 'Yes,' she whispered, her voice a mere thread of sound. 'No one except Jim knows, and now you.'

'Not even Oliver?'

Bron's head flew up, her eyes wide with fright. 'Especially not Oliver. Please, Jesus, don't tell him. . .'

Jesus stared at her for a long time, and then comprehension dawned. 'Oh, my God; he said you'd met before, two years ago—oh, Bron. What possessed you to work here if you didn't want him to know?'

'I didn't know he was here! The last thing I knew, he was in London, at Guy's. My parents live near here, and Mum looks after her. Jesus, please. . .?'

He shook his head as if to clear it, and his troubled eyes swept caringly over her anguished face. 'I won't say a word, Bron, cross my heart. But I think you should tell him—a man has a right to know——'

'What about *my* rights? What about my daughter's rights? Please, Jesus, just leave it alone.'

He nodded. 'OK. But just remember, Bron, I'm here if you need me.'

He unfolded himself from the chair and left the room, patting her shoulder comfortingly on the way past. She poured herself another cup of coffee with shaking hands, and forced it past the growing lump in her throat. She knew she could trust Jesus—but could she trust herself? If he'd been able to read her, wasn't it possible that Oliver could too?

Her throat aching with the effort of holding back the tears, Bron left the sanctuary of the staff-room and threw herself back into the fray.

At five-past one Jim Harris appeared at her side and clamped an arm through hers. 'Lunch,' he said firmly, and she tried to pull away.

'Really, Jim, I'd rather not——'

'Uh-uh. Doctor's orders! Come on.' He walked her relentlessly to the door of the staff-room and stood watching while she shed her white coat, donned her jacket and dragged a comb through her hair. 'Right, you'll do,' he said cheerfully, and, with an avuncular but firm arm around her shoulders, he wheeled her out into the sunshine and across the road to the pub.

The Friday lunchtime session was well under way, with more alcohol than usual flowing on account of baby Marumba's appearance. Bron found a glass of something fizzy thrust in her hand, and wrinkled her nose at the bubbles which tickled it. 'Champagne?' she said in amazement, and Jesus laughed in delight.

'It's not every day I become a dad for the first time!'

Bron smiled at him. 'Here's to your baby—she's very lucky to have a father like you.'

He looked down at her, the pride and happiness on his face tinged with concern, and then he gave her a warm smile and a hug. 'Thank you, Bron.' His voice was rich with emotion, and he cleared his throat self-consciously. 'Crazy, isn't it? I'm torn between laughing and crying. It's—I never realised it would feel so incredible to be a father.'

'Or a mother,' she said softly, for his ears only, and Jesus touched the tip of her nose with his finger.

'May I return the compliment?' he murmured, and she gave him a shaky smile.

'Lighten up, Marumba, or you'll have me in tears with you!' she joked.

He laughed and turned to suffer further back-slapping and congratulations from new arrivals, and Bron was mercifully left alone with her thoughts. Oliver came over and joined her, his face carefully neutral.

'You and Jesus seemed to be having a cosy little chat just now,' he said, and his eyes searched through her, probing deeply. She looked away.

'Just a professional comparing of notes,' she half lied. After all, they had been comparing notes, just not professional ones! God deliver me from intrigue! she thought with desperation, and Jesus appeared at her side, like an answer to her prayer, and started to badger Oliver about visiting Lucy.

'I'll have to pop up this afternoon for a second,' he said. 'Clare's coming for the weekend with a friend, and they're going shopping in Norwich tomorrow. I've promised to have Tom, so I'll be well and truly shackled until Sunday evening. You wait,' he cautioned Jesus, 'once that little bundle of innocence discovers that she can get around, life as you know it will come to an abrupt end. I remember when Tom hauled himself up at the coffee-table and downed half a tumbler of Scotch at a gulp! My God, you don't know you're born at the moment!'

Unable to stand and listen to Oliver regaling Jesus

with stories of his son's misspent toddlerhood, and prevented from joining in with details of his daughter's similar escapades, Bron was only too relieved when her bleep went.

Muttering excuses, she downed her champagne and fled. Technology, she thought as she shut off her bleep. Where would I be without it?

The afternoon passed in the usual blur, and by five o'clock Bron was thoroughly ready to escape.

She let herself into her steaming car, wound down the windows and headed for the exit. She ended up queueing beside Oliver, and he lowered his window and grinned at her.

'How about a walk this weekend? I've got the terror, but we could take him for a ramble in the woods. What do you say?'

She thought of Livvy, left at home so that Bron could go out with her daughter's half-brother and their father, and shook her head. 'Sorry, Oliver. Some other time, maybe.'

His face tightened, and he nodded. The window slid back up with a gentle hiss, and he pulled smoothly away and headed for home, leaving Bron clogging up the traffic and battling with tears.

'I'm going to have my lacrimal glands removed,' she muttered under her breath, and, dashing the tears away, she released the hand-brake and lurched less than smoothly back into the stream of traffic.

Livvy had settled smoothly into their new routine, and she greeted Bron with delight and then carried on stacking a pile of bricks, shrieking with glee when the pile fell on top of her.

''Gain,' she said emphatically, and started patiently

and earnestly re-stacking them. Bron made herself a
cup of tea and sat with her feet tucked up under her,
watching her daughter play. When the last brick was
stacked, Bron clapped loudly and praised her
vigorously.

Livvy's answer was a great swing of her arm, and a
delighted giggle as the bricks tumbled all over the
carpet. Bron swept her up and hugged her, nibbling at
the chubby creases at the side of her neck, so that
Livvy tucked her head in like a tortoise and shrieked
with laughter, offering her neck again as soon as she
could bear it.

She was so like Oliver, Bron thought with a pang,
watching the play of emotions across her little face.
Was Jesus right? Did Oliver have a right to know about
his child?

A nagging voice worried at the back of her mind
while she fed Livvy and prepared her for bed, for once
not soothed by the familiar ritual.

Exhausted by the week, and drained by her
emotions, Bron went herself shortly afterwards, and
then lay, dry-eyed, staring at the ceiling for hours while
she churned over the thoughts in her mind.

Then she turned on her side, curled up and buried
her face in the pillow. Not so many hours ago she had
lain in Oliver's arms as he lay fully dressed on the
covers beside her. That pillow had borne traces of his
scent, unlike this one, which was depressingly familiar
and sterile. A sob rose in her throat, and then the
healing tears came, easing the hurt away and leaving
her exhausted and listless.

She was no nearer to having an answer, but she

couldn't fight her body any longer. Hugging the pillow, she fell into an uneasy and restless sleep.

The next day dawned bright and clear, and Livvy was in fine form. They played together, and fed the ducks on the village pond, and curled up together on the sofa for a sleep in the afternoon. It was a peaceful and beautiful day, and went a long way towards recharging Bron's spirits.

In the evening, old friends of the family came over for a meal, and stayed playing Trivial Pursuit until nearly one in the morning.

Whether it was the hour, or the unaccustomed alcohol, or just the end result of the lovely day, Bron went to bed and slept well, waking to her daughter's chirruping at seven o'clock. She decided to drive into town and go window-shopping, and take Livvy to feed the ducks on the pond in the park. It was the same park that faced Oliver's house, but she thought it unlikely that she would bump into him.

And perhaps it would be just as well if you did, she thought. It would take away the uncertainty, and then you'd have to deal with it.

In the event, though, they didn't bump into Oliver in the park, but what occurred did help Bron to make a decision.

They were feeding the ducks and wandering slowly along beside the pond, Livvy chattering happily to herself, when Bron saw a little fair-haired boy clad in red shorts and a red-and-green striped T-shirt running on the grass ahead of them, a floppy-eared spaniel galloping at his heels. Her heart caught in her throat, and she quickly scanned the area for any sign of Oliver.

There was no trace of him but, as she was turning back, she caught a flash of pale gold, and through the trees she saw a man and a woman walking together, arms linked around each other. The man was dark-haired and well-built, with silvering temples and a Mediterranean tan, and as she watched he pulled the woman into his arms and kissed her thoroughly. She laughed and pushed him away, and he swept her up in his arms and swung her round and round, his head thrown back. A warm, intimate laugh drifted to Bron on the fragrant air, and her heart contracted with pity for that lonely man in the house at the top of the hill. The fool on the hill, she thought, as a cry from the child penetrated the intimate cloud around the couple, breaking their trance.

The man released the woman, and she turned towards her child, confirming what Bron had already guessed from those unforgettable platinum tresses.

It was Clare.

CHAPTER SEVEN

SOMEHOW Bron got home in one piece, although she felt that the world was falling apart all around her. How could she have been such a fool?

For two years, she had protected that faithless woman from hurt, and denied both Oliver and Livvy the opportunity to know and love each other, and now—now was it any different? Perhaps it wasn't what it seemed?

And then she remembered the kiss—that long, slow, thorough kiss. It had been a lovers' kiss, and there was no way round it. She couldn't blame it on anything else, or find any other explanation. There was no hearsay to doubt, no Chinese whispers at work. Hard, blinding evidence that she had seen with her own eyes. Oh, Oliver!

She wondered if he knew. Where was Clare's friend while all this was going on? Perhaps they were sitting in that lovely kitchen with its view of the park waiting for Clare and Tom to come home. Perhaps they were still asleep; perhaps the friend had just been a cover so that Clare and her lover could meet over the weekend—no, ridiculous. Why come and stay up here? Why not stay in London?

It was all getting too complicated, and Bron had a crushing headache by the time she turned into her parents' drive and parked the car. She would have to wait and give herself time to work out what to do—but one thing was sure.

Oliver was going to know that he had a daughter, and that her mother loved him.

The rest of the weekend dragged, and Bron found herself dreading Monday.

In fact it was quiet, and she saw Jesus briefly when she went up to see how Mr Harding was doing. He had made excellent progress, and seemed to be stable now. Perhaps the streptokinase had justified its existence, she thought, and was grateful that modern drugs were available. It must have been hell being a doctor in earlier days before the advent of antibiotics, never mind thrombolytics.

She perched on Mr Harding's bed and chatted to him for a minute or two, and then made her way out of the ward. Jesus appeared at her side with a grin, and displayed a badge that said, 'World's Best Father'.

'How's Lucy?' Bron asked.

'Fine—great. Talking about the next one—you were absolutely right! How are you? You look tired.'

Bron shrugged. 'Not a good weekend.' It suddenly occurred to her that, of all people, she could trust Jesus with her secret fears, but it would be unfair to put him in the position of knowing something about Oliver's wife that not even Oliver knew—if he didn't, which was by no means certain! And Jesus already knew more than was safe about Livvy——

'Penny for them,' Jesus said, dragging her back to reality.

She gave a tiny chuckle. 'No way. You'd have to take out a mortgage to get that lot, and you probably wouldn't make head or tail of it, anyway. Are you going for lunch?'

'Uh-huh. Join me?'

'Sure. I hate eating alone—that's why I asked!'

They met up with Oliver in the queue, and he gave Bron a dirty look and pointedly asked after the new baby.

Jesus launched into a positive litany of tiny toes and night-time feeds, and Bron almost choked on her laughter.

When Jesus was getting another cup of coffee, Oliver fixed her with a keen look, and his mouth tightened in irritation.

'Jesus is a good man, one of my closest friends, and his wife is one of the nicest people I have ever met. I think moving in at this point is the lowest of the low——'

'Just what are you accusing me of?' Bron asked in a voice tight with barely suppressed outrage.

He snorted. 'I would have thought it was obvious!'

Bron got a firm hold on her anger, and stabbed a finger into his chest. 'Listen, Oliver. Jesus Marumba is a friend, got it? F-R-I-E-N-D. No sexual overtones or undercurrents, no innuendo, no snatched kisses. He's offered me friendship—just like you did, only he seems to be making a better job of it than you at the moment!'

His jaw clenched and unclenched, and he opened his mouth and shut it again, and then he sighed heavily. 'I'm sorry,' he muttered. 'That was unforgivable. I know you better than that. It's just that every time I see you with him, I remember—oh, hell. I'm sorry.' His face was bleak, those lovely eyes dull with misery.

Her anger faded, to be replaced by sadness. What

was it that he remembered? Clare's unfaithfulness? Why should he trust Bron? If he couldn't trust Clare, then what made any other woman any different?

She covered his hand, and smiled tentatively at him. 'Forget it. I didn't mean what I said about us, either. I value your friendship very much, Oliver. Just remember, if you ever need me. . .'

He lifted eyes deep with sadness, and swallowed hard. 'Funny you should mention it—are you doing anything tonight? Clare dropped a bombshell on me at the weekend, and I could do with a shoulder to cry on, so to speak.'

Here goes, Bron thought, and forced a smile. 'No, I'm not doing anything.'

'Good. Can you come to the house? I want to get drunk, and I can't do it if I have to drive you.'

'Oliver, that won't help you——'

He snorted. 'It won't stop me trying it. Make it eight—do you feel like picking up a Chinese take-away en route?'

'Fine. I'll see you at the house.' She stood up and straightened her skirt absently. 'Try not to get too drunk before I arrive, hmm?'

He gave her a lop-sided little smile, and she left, waggling her fingers in farewell to Jesus.

All afternoon she pondered his words. Clare had dropped a bombshell—what sort of bombshell? I want to leave you? I'm pregnant and I don't know whose baby it is? I've had an affair and now I want to come back? Impossible to guess, but that didn't stop her trying, all afternoon and evening, so that, by the time she reached his house complete with Chinese take-away at eight, she thought she must have covered all options.

She was wrong, or at least partly, in that nothing she had dreamt up was as cruel as the real thing.

Oliver opened the door, casual and absolutely heart-stopping in beige Chinos and a royal-blue cotton sweater that brought out the colour of his eyes. Bron was glad she had gone to the lengths of wearing a dress—actually the peach tea-dress she had worn on their first evening at the conference, but she didn't expect him to remember it. She had hardly worn it since, because the memories were too vivid, but tonight she felt strong enough to cope.

'Will I pass?' he asked gruffly, and she realised with a start that she had been staring.

'Oh, I reckon—at a pinch!'

He laughed softly and tugged her into his arms, kicking the door shut with his foot.

'You look lovely in that dress. It's how I remember you,' he murmured and, dropping one arm, he brought the other up to her shoulder and steered her through into the kitchen.

The table was set with everyday china, Bron was glad to see, and there were no candles to create an intimate mood. Whatever she might have wondered, he obviously had no great seduction scene in mind. She told herself that she ought to be grateful, and a part of her was relieved but another part, the part that had never really got over him, withered just a little further.

'Red or white?' he asked, and she brought her attention back to him.

'Whatever's open.'

'Red, then.'

'Fine. Thanks.' She took the glass of wine from him,

and noticed that his fingers were trembling. Was it possible that he was nervous?

He eyed her gravely over the carrier-bag. 'Shall we eat now while it's hot?'

She nodded. 'Good idea, I'm starving. I didn't know what you liked, so I got all sorts of things.'

They spread them out on the table and proceeded to sample everything, squabbling like children over the last king prawn and finally sharing it, picking the bits of water-chestnut out and feeding them to each other, and generally eating far too much and still failing to clear the dishes.

'Save it. You can heat it tomorrow.'

'Yuck. We'll come back to it later. Do you want any more now?' Bron shook her head, and Oliver scraped back his chair and went to fill the kettle. 'Go and sit in the drawing-room,' he suggested. 'I'll make coffee. Take your wine.'

Bron decided she'd drunk enough. 'I really shouldn't have more than one glass if I'm driving.'

He nodded and put the glass down. 'OK. You don't mind if I do, do you?'

She shook her head and made her way into the drawing-room, wondering yet again what Clare's bombshell had been.

When Oliver joined her, he set the tray of coffee down on the hearth and sat on the Persian rug, his back against the settee, and patted the rug beside him.

'Come and sit with me. I need that shoulder,' he said, and the weariness in his voice overrode her common sense.

She slid down on the floor beside him and gave him

an encouraging smile. 'You wanted to talk to me,' she prompted gently.

'Mmm. You know I told you Clare was coming for the weekend and bringing a friend? Did I happen to mention that he's six feet two, rich as Croesus and madly in love with her?'

Bron closed her eyes. He sounded so forlorn. 'No, I think I missed that part of the conversation.'

'Well, he is, and Clare's fallen in love with him and wants to marry him. I don't suppose it would be so bad if he didn't live in Sardinia, but he's going to take them both off to the middle of the Mediterranean—oh, Bron, I'll miss them! Especially Tom. You know, when he was born seven weeks early, he had a fractured skull and all sorts of other complications. He had trouble breathing, and he had to be fed hourly through a naso-gastric tube, and he was so pathetic. . .

'I sat beside him for hour after hour, willing him to live, while Clare lay stunned and devastated. I think Tom's death was so shattering to her that she couldn't bring herself to care about the baby, so I took over for a while. I took a month off work to be with him, and it was me who fed him and held his hand and talked to him, me who held him first when he was allowed out of the incubator, me who gave him something to cling to.'

He stopped and closed his eyes, breathing hard, and then continued, 'I don't blame Clare. She couldn't help the way she reacted, but, while she was coming to terms with her grief, that tiny scrap of humanity captured my heart. I love him, Bron, and it's going to kill me when she takes him away——'

His voice broke, and Bron watched in agony as the silent, heavy tears rolled down his cheeks.

'Oh, darling——'

Opening her arms and her heart, she pulled his head down on to her breast and cradled it with her hands, murmuring soothing, timeless words while her own tears flowed unheeded from her eyes. His body shook with huge, racking sobs as he let go of the pain, and she clung tightly to him, waiting patiently as the storm passed and he grew quiet and still in her arms.

After an age he straightened up, propped his elbows on his knees and his head in his hands.

'I'm sorry, Bron. I don't know what made me do that.'

'Shh. Have a cup of coffee.' She sat forward and poured two cups, and handed him one.

He grimaced and took it from her, eyeing her face searchingly. 'You cried,' he whispered, and she nodded.

'Of course. It hurts me to see you like this.'

'Oh, Bron. . .' He took her hand in his and laced his fingers through hers. 'Thanks for being here for me, and not making me feel an idiot.'

She smiled shakily. 'You're welcome.' She sipped her coffee, and, pulling a face, put it back on the tray. 'It's cold. I'll make some more——'

'No.' He caught her wrist with his hand, and pulled her back to his side. 'Stay here with me. Just sit here and let me hold you—no strings, I promise.'

She put her head on his shoulder and laid a hand over his heart. She wondered if they ever really broke. Sometimes it felt very much like it. She could feel his hand against her back, moving comfortingly against her spine, and she sighed and snuggled into him.

'It was wonderful sleeping with you on Thursday night,' he said softly into her hair, and she lifted her head to look at him.

'I'm not sure we ought to do it again, Oliver. Someone might see us——'

'Who cares?'

'I do!' she protested.

'I don't—but I won't come down again. You're probably right. Bron?'

She dropped her head back on to his shoulder. 'Mmm?'

She felt his fingers cup her chin and lift it, and watched, spellbound, as his lips lowered to cover hers with a feather-light caress.

She gave a little moan, either of protest or longing, and he crushed her closer, his lips tormenting, the velvet warmth of his tongue seeking hers and, finding it, caressing it delicately until the heat flared between them again. Then he shifted her until she lay beneath him, and, while one hand tangled intimately in the hair at her nape, the other hand moved surely down from her shoulder across the slope of her breast, to cup its warm fullness in the palm. She squirmed against him, desperate for his touch all over her, aching with a terrible emptiness that only he could fill.

His lips moved to her hair, and he groaned against its softness.

'Oh, Bron, I want you so much—it's been so long. . .'

So long since he had made love to her? Or Clare? With a sickening chill, she reminded herself that he was still married, whatever might happen in the future. Things could change. Clare's rich lover could fade into oblivion, and then where would they all be?

If it was hard to work with Oliver now, how much harder if she had slept with him again and then Clare had come back to him?

Taking a deep breath, she pushed gently on his chest, and turned her head away from his questing lips.

'No, Oliver. Please. You promised. . .'

He stilled, and then groaned. 'I'm sorry. I didn't mean to do this. I guess it's just been one of those evenings. Forgive me?'

'Of course I forgive you.'

He laid a gentle, passionless kiss on her lips and smiled ruefully. 'Coffee?'

She smiled back. 'I think so—strong and black! And then I must go.'

'Yes, I think you must. Come and drink it in the kitchen. I'm less likely to be tempted there.'

He kept a safe distance from her on the way to the kitchen, and then sat on the opposite side of the table, picking at the cold remains of the Chinese meal.

'You'll get fat,' she scolded, and he grinned.

'Don't care. I like picking the prawns out of the rice.'

'Prawns? Where?' Bron dived in and helped him finish them, and then, meeting his eyes, she stood reluctantly.

'I must go now.'

He nodded, and followed her to the front door, pausing before he opened it.

'Thank you for coming over this evening, Bron. I'm sorry—about everything.'

He wrapped her carefully in his arms, and hugged her tight. 'You're one in a million, do you know that?'

'You're pretty special, too,' she whispered and, reaching up, she pulled his face down and kissed him. 'Goodnight, Oliver. Sweet dreams.'

'And you. Drive carefully.'

She buckled herself into her seat and started the car, glancing back as she turned into the road. His arm was lifted in farewell, and a sad little smile was playing around his lips.

How could Clare do that to him? Bron wondered, agonising for him during the endless days and nights that followed.

Occasionally she saw him briefly, but she maintained the distance for fear of weakening her resolve. Until their divorce was sorted out and final, until there was no possibility of her influencing the break-up of his marriage, she would keep her distance, even if it killed her.

There were days, of course, when she was sure it would, but the nights on call were the hardest. During the second night on, about ten days after his shattering revelation, they were forced to work together over and over again, and by the morning she was ready to scream with anguish.

He had been tireless, thoughtful and understanding with his patients, co-operative and undemanding with the staff, and, despite the repeated demands on him, he had remained quietly competent in the face of utter mayhem.

Professional admiration on top of her already raging emotions just made it harder to distance herself from him, and, when he lost a patient and she saw the anguish and frustration in his eyes, she almost gave in to the urge to comfort him. Instead she sat down and rubbed his shoulders to ease the tension, and sent him back to Theatre even more frustrated by the unsatisfactory contact.

At lunchtime she went to the pub for her usual fruit juice and salad, and to her disappointment Oliver wasn't there. Not that she wanted to see him, exactly, but she couldn't bear it if she didn't.

Once or twice she caught Jesus watching her, and she wasn't surprised when he came down in midafternoon and cornered her in the staff-room.

'What's up, Bron?' he asked with characteristic directness, and she shrugged her shoulders and turned away.

'Nothing. I'm just tired. We had a hell of a night.'

'Don't lie, Bron. It's Oliver, isn't it? You love him, don't you?'

She sat down abruptly and burst into tears. 'Oh, Jesus, I've tried, really I have. So has he. But it's so *hard* to be detached, especially when I can see him hurting so much inside.'

'Has he told you about Clare?' he asked, and she nodded and lifted her tear-stained face.

'Jesus, how can she *do* that to him? How will he cope without them? He loves that child so much, it's going to break his heart not to see him any more. Oh, the bitch!'

'Hey, hey! That's a bit strong! Bron, she deserves her happiness like anyone else. She's suffered so much, and Oliver's really pleased for her. She was so broken up when Tom died, and I think he thought she'd never find anyone else, but this guy really seems to love her, and he's devoted to Tom. The child needs a father——'

'But he's got a father!'

Jesus shook his head. 'No, Bron, he's got a devoted uncle who's done his best to fill the gap, but it's not the same, and it never can be. Tom needs a real father, and Clare needs a husband. However much support Oliver's given her, and I'll admit he's been fantastic, it can't be the same. And it's hampered Oliver's social life, too. He needs a chance—maybe with you?'

Bron stared at Jesus as if he were talking utter gibberish. 'I don't understand. What are you talking about?'

Jesus frowned at her. 'What do you mean? What's so complicated about it? The man's done everything that could be asked of him, and more, to help his sister get over her bereavement, but now it's time to move on. Of course it'll be a wrench to hand over the responsibility, but in many ways he's relieved—Bron, what is it?'

'But—Clare's his wife——'

'No, she's not—she's his twin sister.'

'But she can't be!' Bron cried. 'The receptionist said his brother-in-law had been killed and his wife was pregnant. . .' Slowly, realisation dawned. 'Tom's wife. Jesus, I thought he was married. For two years, I've thought he was married—that's why I wouldn't tell him about the baby, because I didn't want to risk breaking up their marriage—and all the time I had got hold of the wrong end of the stick! Oh, God, what a waste!'

Jesus looked stunned. 'Oh, Bron. You must have been through hell. Look, tell him about the baby, about the misunderstanding, all of it. Tell him now, today. Don't keep it from him, I beg you. He loves you, Bron, he's told me. He thinks you've got a lover.'

She shook her head, her face clearing miraculously. 'No, I haven't, but I soon will have.' She leapt to her feet and seized him by the hands, and he stood and smiled down at her. Neither of them noticed the door open as Bron laughed exultantly. 'Oh, Jesus, I love you!'

She flung her arms around his neck and hugged him tight, and he bent his head and gave her a brotherly kiss.

'My God!' The door closed with a vicious slam, and Jesus stepped away from Bron and closed his eyes.

'That's torn it. You stay here; I'll go and find him and explain.'

But Oliver had left the hospital, and was apparently spending the weekend in London. He returned in the middle of the following week, and cold-shouldered Bronwen whenever they had to meet.

Only the pain written clearly in his eyes helped to soften her anger at his refusal to listen, so she decided to allow him to burn himself out. What she had to say was too important to squeeze into a hurried coffee-break, and, the way he was carrying on, he wasn't going to listen anyway.

By Friday she was at breaking-point, and was only too relieved when an emergency required her attention at five to one.

At a quarter past, Oliver appeared at her elbow, smiled vaguely at the patient and muttered, 'We need to talk, Bron.'

'You're telling me, but now is not the time.'

She continued stitching up the torn skin of the patient's forearm, while Oliver crossed his arms over his chest and watched with professional interest as she drew the damaged tissues together.

'You're good. Why don't you go into surgery?'

'Because I find it too traumatic. Pass me the scissors, please.' She clipped the sutures, peeled off her gloves and dropped them into the bin, and turned back to her patient. 'All right, Mr Braithwaite? You'll have to take it easy for a few days, now, and either come back here or go to your GP to have the stitches out in a week. OK?'

She helped the elderly man off the couch and escorted him through the door. Oliver followed her, altogether too distractingly good-looking in his suit and dark Paisley tie, and she shoved her hands into her pockets and turned to face him.

'Coffee?' she asked tersely, and he nodded.

'Thanks.'

He followed her into the staff-room in silence and watched as she made the coffee, and then stirred it until she sighed with irritation.

'Oliver, you don't take sugar.'

He lifted puzzled eyes to her face. 'What? Oh, that——' He returned the spoon to the saucer, and set the cup down on the table.

'Bron, Jesus cornered me this morning.'

'Oh, yes? Did he tell you how our affair is progressing?'

Oliver ran irritated fingers through his hair and sighed. 'Damn it, Bron, you can't blame me for thinking what I did.'

'Why not? I told you we were just friends—anyway, he's not my type.'

'Why? Because he's black?' Perversely, he now sounded angry that she would *not* choose his friend.

Bron laughed. 'No. Actually, I find him very attractive, and that wouldn't matter to me at all. No, because he's married. I don't tangle with married men, Oliver. I've told you that before, too.' She paused. 'So what did he tell you?'

Oliver shrugged. 'He said I'd have to ask you, but that he thought you'd found out something that would make a difference to us; I don't know, he was talking in riddles.'

'Maybe, but he's right. I did find out something, and it does make a difference—it makes an enormous difference.'

'So much difference that you'll let me take you out? There's a Royal Medical Benevolent Fund charity ball tomorrow night that I have to put in an appearance at. Will you come with me? We can talk afterwards. I got the tickets last week—that's what I was coming to tell you last Friday when I caught you and Jesus tangled in that clinch——'

'It wasn't a clinch! And yes, I'd love to come with you. Is it frightfully grand?'

'Oh, frightfully!' he said with a smile. 'Is that a problem?'

Bron shook her head and her eyes danced. 'No way. I'm going shopping tomorrow, for a ball-gown!'

The loudspeaker on the wall squawked her name, and she gave a rueful shrug. 'Duty calls. By the way——'

'Yes?'

'I love you.'

She walked quietly away, her feet floating just above the ground, and left Oliver speechless, wrapped around by the sound of her soft laughter.

'How do I look?'

Bron twirled, and the full skirt of her deep-rose taffeta gown swirled out around her calves. Her feet were clad in tiny black sandals, and the low, scooped neck of the bodice showed off her slim shoulders to perfection.

Her mother was clearly moved. 'Lovely, darling. Absolutely stunning. Oh, Bron, I'm so happy for you!'

Bron hugged her parents, dodged Livvy's sticky fingers and bent to kiss her goodnight.

'Be a good girl for Mummy, won't you?' she said, and, picking up her shawl and bag, she let herself out and climbed carefully into her car. She had insisted on going to Oliver's house, because he was on call for dire emergencies if his registrar couldn't cope, and she didn't want to be stranded. However, his house was between the hotel where the ball was being held and the hospital, so if necessary he could drop her there without wasting any time.

Suppressing her nerves, she started the car and drove carefully towards the town, turning into his drive at ten to eight.

He wrenched the door open with an exasperated scowl on his face, and she hid her smile. He looked immaculate in a black dinner-jacket, with a sparkling white tucked shirt and rich burgundy cummerbund, the satin stripe down the outside of his trousers gleaming in the evening sun. The only sour note was the bow-tie, which he said had refused all his efforts to tie it, and which now hung bedraggled against his shirt-front.

'Let me,' she offered, and he bent his knees so that she could reach better while she tied it.

'There.' She patted it, and then looked at him. 'Very dashing. Remind me to tell you some time how very handsome you are, Mr Henderson.'

'Thank you, Dr Jones,' he murmured with a smile, and stepped away to walk all round her. He gave a low whistle of admiration.

'Bron, you look beautiful. Did you buy that just for tonight?'

She pouted. 'Do you mean you aren't ever going to take me out again?'

He grinned and tugged her into his arms. 'No way. Are you going to tell me this amazing thing you've found out?'

'Later. There's too much to say and, if I start now, we won't get to the ball, and that would be a terrible waste of a dress!'

'In that case,' he muttered, reaching for his keys, 'let's get out of here before my baser nature gets the better of me!'

He opened the front door for her, then the car door, seating her with old-fashioned courtesy before closing the door and sliding in beside her. As she settled back against the soft grey leather upholstery, he started the car, put in into gear, and then cut the engine.

'Have you forgotten something?'

He laughed softly. 'More of an oversight. Yesterday you sashayed out of the staff-room with one hell of a parting shot—I'd just like to check it out. . .'

His firm, warm fingers snaked out and captured her chin, and he dragged his thumb slowly across her full lips. As her breath caught in her throat, he lowered his head and touched his mouth to hers with exquisite care. She moaned and reached up to his face, but he moved out of range and his warm laugh floated round her like a sensuous wave.

'Later,' he whispered, and the promise in his eyes brought a glow to her cheeks, and a surge of warmth to her heart.

CHAPTER EIGHT

THEY arrived at the hotel at the same time as Jesus and Lucy Marumba, and they all made their way together to the bar. Oliver went off to find some drinks, and Lucy went to the ladies' to repair her make-up, leaving Bron alone with Jesus.

He gave her a look of wholly masculine appraisal, and followed it with a warm, open smile that lit up his face.

'You look beautiful, Bron. For the first time in ages, you look at peace with yourself. Have you told him?'

She shook her head. 'No, but I will tonight. Jesus, I'm scared. I feel such a fool——'

'No. You aren't a fool. You did a very courageous thing, carrying that responsibility in the light of what you thought was the truth. I have only admiration for you. Don't be scared. He'll understand, Bron. He's a good man, and he'll be over the moon to know he's a father. Just give him time to come to terms with it, if necessary, but I doubt if it will be. Good luck, anyway.'

He reached out and squeezed her hand, and she returned the pressure.

'Thank you, Jesus. You've been so kind——'

'Hey, Marumba, that's my woman. Put her down!'

Jesus laughed easily and leaned back in his chair. 'Jealous, old boy? I can assure you, all she talks about is you, *ad nauseam*. In fact, you're well matched. I just wish you'd talk to each other and leave out the middle-man.'

'We intend to,' Oliver said with quiet certainty. 'There are a lot of things I wanted to say two years ago. It's time I got them off my chest.'

Lucy returned then, sparing Bron the problem of carrying on what was fast becoming a difficult conversation. The men both stood, and, as Jesus hovered solicitously around his wife, the current that passed between them made Bron look quickly away. Really, she thought, if Oliver only had eyes in his head he'd know that Jesus is head over heels in love with his wife.

After giving them a second or two of privacy, Bron turned to Lucy and asked after the baby.

'She's wonderful. So easy. I love her to bits. The only problem is that we can't agree on a name——'

'Just because you're so stubborn and won't let me have my way!' Jesus complained, and Lucy retaliated, eyes flashing. They entered into another round of what was obviously a long-standing and favourite feud, and Oliver lounged back in his seat and watched them both fondly.

Bron caught his eye, and he winked. 'OK?' he mouthed, and she nodded.

'Oh, shut up, darling,' Jesus said eventually, and silenced his wife by the simple expedient of planting a long and extremely expressive kiss on her lips.

Oliver cleared his throat, and they tore themselves reluctantly apart.

'Disgusting. Some people don't know how to behave,' he murmured under his breath, and Jesus answered with a laugh.

'Some people are too staid for their own good,' he

replied cheerfully, and turned to Lucy. 'Shall we show these two how it's done?' he suggested, and she rose gracefully.

'Just bear in mind that Jessica is only three weeks old——'

'Elizabeth!'

'Whatever. Come on, then, Casanova, the night is young. Let's boogie!'

Which they did, very successfully, on an almost empty dance-floor, until gradually their infectious good spirits encouraged others to join them.

'Shall we?' Oliver asked, and held out his hand to Bron.

'Why not?' She linked her fingers through his for the short distance to the dance-floor, and then, as if by conspiracy, the band changed the mood with a slow, intimate number, dimming the lights accordingly.

'No, I didn't bribe them,' Oliver said with a chuckle, and drew Bron into his arms.

As his hand passed warmly against her spine, she felt all the old familiar feelings come flooding back. It was as if they had never been apart, as if they had travelled back in time to the party at the conference—before the horrendous events of that night had ripped them apart and flung them to opposite corners of the country. . .before Livvy, before Tom, before anything had had time to intervene and trample their fragile love underfoot.

And yet here they were, two years and so much emotion later, about to come out of the tunnel—together.

With a small sigh of contentment, Bron laid her

cheek against Oliver's shoulder and let the feelings wash over her.

When the music speeded up, they ignored it and halved the tempo, and, when the chairman of the local branch of the RMBV stood up to make a speech thanking everyone for their generosity, and telling them that the buffet was open should they care to go and investigate, they merely paused as they were, and waited for the music to start again.

They danced through supper, and then, when the dance-floor became crowded again, they worked their way slowly and steadily through the undulating bodies to the french doors and out on to the terrace.

There, in a tiny area of shadow between two sets of doors, Oliver pulled her closer and lowered his lips to hers, kindling the flickering flames to a raging inferno. She could feel his heart thundering against her breasts and, as he urged her closer still, she felt the hard thrust of his desire against her soft flesh.

A low moan escaped her, and he gentled the kiss instantly, teasing and tormenting her until she felt boneless with longing.

Then he lifted his head and stared down at her with storm-tossed eyes that held a message older than time. His voice was a harsh, ragged whisper against her hair. 'Bron, I need you so badly. It's been two long years—don't make me wait any more. . .'

Bron was helpless against the pleading in his voice and the clamouring of her own heart, and she knew the time had come.

'Do you think you could hang on until we find somewhere rather more private?' she said a little breathlessly, and he gave a short, tortured laugh and eased away from her slightly.

'Fine. Give me a minute to get respectable, and we'll go.'

'Do you need to?' she asked. 'We could walk round to the car park without going back in.'

'What about your shawl?'

Bron shrugged. 'Oliver, just at the moment I think it's a small sacrifice to pay for being alone with you, but if you like I'll go and get it and meet you at the car.'

'Where are your car keys?'

'Oh. In my bag with my shawl—I'll get them. Wait here.' She worked her way quickly through the crowd, and retrieved her things just as Jesus and Lucy were making their way out.

He wished her luck in an undertone, and then she made her way back through the crowd to the terrace.

'Got them?'

She nodded, and, tucking her into his side, Oliver led her round to the car park and settled her into the passenger-seat. Then he crossed round and slid in beside her in silence, and, as he drove, the tension built to screaming-pitch between them.

Bron was aware of every hair on his hands, every blink of his eyes, the slightest shift of muscle in his legs. It was the longest twenty minutes of her life, and, as they turned into the drive of his house and he cut the engine, she almost laughed out loud with relief.

'Come on,' he said gruffly, and took her arm to help her from the car. The warmth of his fingers against the cool skin of her upper arm made her weak with longing, and she swayed against him, turning her face blindly to his shoulder for support.

He slammed the car door and swept her up into his arms, unlocking the front door and pushing it open without lowering her to the ground, and then, kicking the door shut behind him, he carried her tenderly up the stairs.

He shouldered open the door of his bedroom, and lowered her at last to the soft welcome of a lovely old four-poster bed. Then he sank down beside her and stared at her as if he found it hard to believe she was real.

'I've pictured you here so many times in the last few weeks,' he said hoarsely, running his fingers unsteadily through her hair to fan it on the pillow. 'You're so beautiful—oh, Bron, I love you so much.'

'Make love to me, Oliver—please?'

'Oh, yes, my darling. It'll be a pleasure.'

He rolled her over and eased the zip down on her dress, and then slid the shoulders down slowly, puzzled when he met the resistance of the boned bodice. 'How does this thing come off?' he asked pleadingly, and Bron laughed low in her throat and slipped off the other side of the bed.

Then she undressed for him, watching him as she lowered the dress to reveal nothing but a fine silk teddy clinging softly to her gentle curves.

'Oh, my God,' he breathed, and then closed his eyes briefly as she unfastened the suspenders and peeled her stockings down one by one.

She watched the rise and fall of his chest, and the tension mounted between them until their breathing was the only sound in the room, harsh and ragged, all attempt at playfulness abandoned.

Then he reached his hand up and tugged his bow-tie free, throwing it aside, and following it with the jacket and the cummerbund. The shirt followed more slowly, and then he kicked off his shoes, and the trousers, briefs and socks joined them in one rapid movement.

Moving slowly round the end of the bed, he held out his hand to her and she placed her own trustingly in the cradle of his palm. He closed his fingers over it and drew her gently to him, catching his breath as their bodies swayed together, and then he lifted her and laid her gently in the centre of the bed.

If she hadn't loved him so much and needed him so badly, the raw emotion carved into his features would have terrified her. As it was, she was simply reassured that the shattering sensations sweeping through her like wildfire were burning him up as well. And yet, despite the heat of their passion, he was unfailingly gently, although his body shook with the effort to control it.

Just when she thought the wait was ended, he lifted himself away from her, stilling her questing hands. 'Bron, wait. Is it OK? Are you on the Pill?'

Numbly, she shook her head. How could he think of things like that now? Then he was reaching for his bedside table, and she closed her eyes. The irony of it hit her with blinding force so that she almost gave in to the hysterical urge to laugh.

'It's OK now,' he murmured, turning back to her. 'I'd hate you to get pregnant just yet. I want you to myself for a while.'

Tell him, her mind screamed, but her body's voice

was louder, and, with a soft cry, she yielded to his tender thrust.

Oh, and it was wonderful to feel his body again, to touch and hold and welcome him to her citadel, and, as he brought all his power and tenderness to bear on her, she spiralled higher even than before; clinging, sobbing, to the sweat-slicked skin of his back, she felt the world fall away as he drove into her one last time and collapsed against her, her name a fierce cry on his lips.

As their harsh breathing slowed and steadied, she lifted her hand and smoothed the hair from his brow, laying a tender kiss on the damp skin.

'I love you,' she whispered, and he opened his eyes and stared deep into her soul.

'I love you too, Bron. I always have.' His lids closed again, but not before Bron saw the fleeting shadow that writhed behind his eyes.

'Why didn't you reply to my letters?' he asked in a strained voice, and Bron's heart quailed at the sound of so much pain.

Time to talk, she thought, and took a slow, steadying breath.

'When I got up that morning, I found your note saying that you had so much to tell me, and that you had slept in your room because you didn't want any speculation. Then, when I went downstairs, the manager found me and told me you'd been called away. His actual words were, "His brother-in-law was killed in a car accident. He said his wife Clare was pregnant, and he had to be with her."'

Oliver gave her a puzzled frown. 'So?'

'So I thought Clare was *your* wife, and that you'd

gone back to your room because you didn't want any speculation about yourself, not me. I thought the things you had to tell me were that you were going home to your pregnant wife. Oliver, I thought I was going to die of misery!' she cried brokenly.

'Oh, my love—but you must have realised when you read my letters——'

'But that's just it, Oliver. I didn't read them! I was so hurt and confused by what I had misunderstood, that when you eventually deigned to put pen to paper I was too upset and angry to read them. I just chucked them in the bin, unopened.'

'Oh, Bron!' He pulled her into his arms, and cradled her head on his chest, smoothing her hair back tenderly. 'So when *did* you realise?'

She laughed shakily. 'Last week.'

'Not till then? I don't believe it—so all this talk about going home to someone who loved you was just hogwash to throw me off the scent?'

She debated with the truth, and erred on the side of cowardice. 'More or less,' she agreed.

'That's incredible. So what made you realise, in the end?'

'You told me Clare was marrying this friend, and I was so hurt and angry for you that I was practically out of control. Then Jesus caught up with me and I raged at him about the way she was treating you and how heartbroken you would be to lose Tom, and he couldn't see what I was getting at until he let slip about your being a devoted uncle—then everything began to fall into place.'

'And that's when I walked in—oh, Bron, my poor

darling. All these wasted years. How could you believe I would do that?'

'I couldn't—that's why it hurt so badly, I think, to know that I was such a rotten judge of character. I can't tell you how wonderful it is to know that you aren't a lousy rat, after all!'

He laughed, and his breath stirred her hair, lifting it away from her face and revealing her love to him.

Then the laughter stopped in his throat, and he raised himself up on one elbow and looked down at her in wonder.

'Oh, darling, I don't care how long it's taken; you're with me now, where you belong.' His head came down, blocking out the rest of the world, and his lips told her of his love more eloquently than any speech.

This time their passion was less demanding, and they made love slowly, with great care and tenderness, laughing softly and teasing with great affection, until the fire caught them up and drove them before it into a burning wilderness where only lovers could survive.

As their love-damp skin cooled, Oliver lifted Bron and tucked her under the quilt, sliding in beside her and wrapping her in the safety of his warm embrace. Then, together at last, they slept the sleep of the innocent.

They were awoken a short while later by fireworks in the park opposite, and they sat up in bed and watched the colourful display.

'Noisy, aren't they?' he murmured. 'They do this every year. I expect there's been a fair or something.'

He went down to the kitchen and returned with a tray of cheese and biscuits, fruit cake and coffee.

'That's really going to help us sleep!' Bron teased.

'So who wants to sleep?'

She saw the warm twinkle in his eye, and caught her lower lip between her teeth. Really, she thought, she must tell him about Livvy before she allowed him to side-track her any further. But how to phrase it? Listen, Oliver, about wanting me to yourself for a while—I'm afraid you're two years too late to worry about taking precautions? Or how about, You know you're losing Tom? Well, you've gained a daughter instead. How does that grab you?

She groaned and reached for another piece of fruit cake. If only she had taken the opportunity when it presented itself—but she knew realistically that then had not been the right time. So what was?

Deciding that there was no easy way round it, she laid the fruit cake down and took a deep breath.

'Oliver, there's something else——'

'What in the name of God was that?' Oliver shot out of bed just as a deafening roar hit the house, shaking the windows and rattling the doors. A huge sheet of flame rose up in the sky and, over the tremendous sound of exploding fireworks, they heard the first screams start.

'Bloody hell! The main cache of fireworks must have gone up.' Oliver's voice was faint with shock. 'Come on, Bron, they'll need us.'

He snatched open a drawer and tugged out jeans and a sweatshirt, and dragged them on, not bothering with underwear.

'I can't wear my dress,' she said, suddenly helpless, and he looked up from fastening his shoes and paused.

'Clare might have left something here—a jogging-suit or something. Come on.'

Bron ran after him into another room. 'Here,' he said tersely, thrusting a handful of clothes at her. 'Get something on. I'll be in the study.'

He threw himself downstairs four at a time, and seconds later she could hear him talking to ambulance control, and then rousing Jim Harris and alerting the A and E department. She heard the words 'Major Incident Contingency Plan' as she was pushing her feet into a pair of trainers. Fortunately Clare's feet seemed to be about the same size.

Bron ran downstairs. 'I'm ready. Is there anything we need to take?'

He shook his head. 'Only my cellphone so I can keep in touch with HQ. Come on.'

They ran out of the house, slamming the door to behind them, and sprinted across the road. Oliver hoisted Bron over the railings and then vaulted them, and, grabbing her hand, he towed her across the park towards the scene of the explosion.

Fireworks were still going off spasmodically, and as they approached they were greeted by a scene of carnage beyond anything Bron had ever experienced. Bodies lay scattered everywhere—some dead, some horribly injured, and people were panicking and running in circles trying to find loved ones. Over all hung a pall of yellow smoke, acrid with the smell of sulphur and something else she couldn't identify.

'What's that awful smell?' she asked him.

He swallowed. 'Burning flesh. It's not going to be nice, Bron—can you cope?'

She nodded, and took several deep breaths. 'OK. Where do we start?'

Oliver waded into the crowd, and somehow managed to locate the microphone for the public-address system. Using it, he managed to calm the crowd, and, as an uneasy silence fell, punctuated only by the sobs of terrified youngsters and the moans of the injured, he explained that medical help was on its way. 'Please, if you've been hurt, just sit down quietly, and someone will come and help you as soon as it's humanly possible. If there are any people in the crowd trained in first aid, or with any medical qualification, could you come over here so that we can co-ordinate? Thank you.'

He shut off the microphone and turned to the St John's Ambulance volunteer beside him. 'What have you got in the way of first-aid kit?'

The man looked out across the crowd, and shook his head numbly. 'Damn all, for this lot. Apparently someone broke into the steel box and poured petrol on the fireworks, and then lit a fuse.'

Oliver's face grew even grimmer. 'OK, let's get to work.'

Afterwards, Bron would have given almost anything to be able to erase the memories of that terrible night. They worked automatically, soothing and comforting, treating shock and splinting broken limbs, but above all trying to deal with the terrible burns which were the majority of injuries.

Occasionally Bron caught a glimpse of Oliver's face as he moved from casualty to casualty, rapidly assessing the seriousness of their injuries and establishing a priority for removal to hospital.

The first ambulances on the scene brought, as

instructed, quantities of saline for irrigation of the burns and also for setting up IV lines where necessary. They also brought pain-relief, and, as Oliver moved among the most severely injured, setting up drips and administering pain-killing injections, gradually the haunting animal cries died away to low moans.

He appeared by her side to give morphine to one young man who had lost all the skin on his face and hands, and much on his arms and chest. He was wearing a T-shirt in man-made fibres, and it had melted in pools on his skin. Bron was dribbling saline steadily over the burns, but his condition was critical and he was going into shock fast.

'Help him, Oliver,' she begged, and he nodded. Eventually he found a vein that might take the giving set, and swabbed it down.

'Hold him still,' he murmured, and, as he got the line set up and the drug took effect, the terrible keening died away to a low, tortured groan.

'Why are burns so painful?' she asked, near to tears, and in reply he squeezed her shoulder and moved on to the next victim.

The ambulance crew removed her patient and she transferred her attention to another youth who had also caught the blast, although with less disastrous results. As she worked, she became aware of another figure in the crowd, and looked up to find the gynae SHO she had criticised so severely rolling up his sleeves and pitching in, a look of anguish on his face.

Good, she thought, that'll knock some sense into him!

Gradually the injured were removed to hospital, and

the bodies of those arguably less fortunate were borne away for identification.

'Eight dead, something over sixty injured, eleven critically,' Oliver intoned beside her, 'and all because some stupid bastard decided to pull a damn-fool stunt like that!' His voice shook with rage, and he pulled Bron roughly into his arms.

'Well done, darling. You were marvellous,' he murmured into her hair, and she wrapped her arms tight around his waist and clung to him.

The shock was hitting her now, and she could hardly manage the walk back to Oliver's house. Once there, they took it in turns to shower and change, and then they went in convoy to the hospital. While Oliver went to scrub up for Theatre, Bron, in her borrowed clothes, continued with the work of admitting the serious patients and attending to the others, sending them home with pain-killers and instructions, and dealing with distraught relatives.

Finally they were finished, and, as she hung up her white coat and rounded up her car keys, she wondered how Oliver was doing.

Her clothes were still all over his bedroom floor, and she wondered what her mother would make of her appearance in someone else's clothes.

Too tired to worry, she made her way to her car just as the rain started to fall. It was going to be a grey, dismal day—a fitting memorial to those who had died that night.

She fell into bed in a tangle of exhausted limbs, and her sleep was tormented by cries of pain and tear-streaked faces, injured children holding out their arms for love and reassurance, and, in the distance, a youth whose cruel laughter turned to screams as the flames engulfed him.

It was only when she woke, physically refreshed but mentally devastated, that she remembered she still hadn't told Oliver about his daughter.

CHAPTER NINE

BRON rang Oliver at midday to see how he was, and got the answer-phone. She debated leaving a message, and in the end just said, 'I love you,' and hung up.

Her mother forced her to eat, and her father listened with grim sympathy as she recounted the events of the night.

'Oliver was fantastic,' she said quietly, and closed her eyes to conjure up again the vision of him moving quietly and confidently among the victims.

A shudder racked her, and her father drew his brows together into a frown and sent her back to bed with a mild sedative.

This time she slept peacefully, and when she woke her mother told her that Oliver had phoned.

'He almost insisted on coming round, but I think I managed to stall him. I wasn't sure if you'd told him about Livvy yet.'

Bron shook her head. 'I was just about to, when the fireworks went up,' she explained. 'I just didn't know how to put it, and now I think I've lost my nerve.'

Her mother patted her hand reassuringly. 'Don't worry, darling. The right time will come.'

But somehow it never did.

Monday saw an almost party atmosphere descend on the department as they praised each other and themselves for the success of the contingency plans. Bron, particularly, came in for much unstinted praise from

Jim Harris and the rest of the team, and gradually her spirits were restored and the spectre of the carnage was driven back.

Of Oliver there was no sign, and Bron began to wonder if the miracle of their lovemaking had been part of a dream, all part and parcel of the nightmare of the firework display. Perhaps that had been an omen, she thought, but his intimate phone call later in the evening drove away the insidious suggestion.

On Tuesday Oliver shot down to A and E and cornered her for a brief kiss and a much-needed hug in the staff-room before dashing away again in answer to his bleep.

On Wednesday he was operating as usual, and on Thursday she was too busy to pause for breath. It was her night on and, as she went mechanically from one patient to another throughout the long and busy night, she wondered if she would ever have time to stand still long enough to talk to him.

Friday was hell, as usual, and she was too tired and too busy to go over to the pub. Oliver was in Theatre, in any case, and was away for the weekend in London, meeting Clare's fiancé's family.

She began to ask herself how they would ever keep their relationship going, when it was based on snatched kisses and ten-second conversations.

The weekend was long and intolerably lonely without even so much as a glimpse of him, and she took Livvy to feed the ducks and then killed a little more time at the swings. They bought an ice-cream and shared it messily, and Bron was reminded of the picture of Tom on Oliver's kitchen wall.

'You've got a little cousin just like you,' she said

with a lump in her throat, and wiped the mess up with
a tissue. Livvy protested violently, and so Bron gave in
and left her, sticky and content, while they walked
through the arboretum and back to the car.

She avoided the area of the firework display, and
drove home fighting the loneliness that threatened to
swamp her.

She went out with friends that evening, and they
went to a film and on to a wine-bar afterwards. Bron
left them early, unable to enjoy herself without him,
and went home and cried herself to sleep.

She didn't mean to. She knew that they would soon
be together, but she missed the feel of his arms around
her and the beat of his heart, steady under her ear.

Oliver was missing Bron damnably. The weekend away
had seemed interminable, and he drove to the hospital
with unusual enthusiasm, even for him. Maybe today
he would find time to catch up with Bron and ask her
to marry him.

When he had told Clare about her, she had delved
in her jewellery-box and come up with an old family
ring. 'Granny's engagement ring,' she told him. 'Go
home and ask her to marry you, and get her to move
in with you now before you forget what she looks like!'

'I'll never forget what she looks like,' he had replied
with devastating simplicity, and, pocketing the ring, he
had returned late on Sunday night, full of joy and hope
and love.

Now he was on the way to the hospital, and would
see her at last.

He called in at A and E, but she was busy with a
patient, so, resolving to come down again later, he

made his way to the wards and did the rounds with the sister, chatting reassuringly with the patients who were on his list for the afternoon.

The last patient was an elderly woman with a rectal abscess, who was having a temporary colostomy to allow the abscess to clear. When he had examined her, he covered her up, and then perched on the end of her bed with her notes.

'Now, Mrs Bright,' he said, 'after this is all over, the nurse at your general practice will be able to help you with the care of your colostomy if you feel you can't manage it. I'll be writing to your GP and filling him in, so he'll be out to look at you, too. OK?'

'Oh, yes,' she replied, 'I'm sure they'll take very good care of me, doctor. They always do, there. Dr Jones is a marvellous GP—one of the old sort, I always think. A real family doctor. I expect you know his daughter, too, don't you? She works here now, I believe, so Winnie at the post office was saying. In Casualty, or something.'

'Yes, that's right,' he nodded. 'Yes, I know her. Excellent doctor.' And a wonderful lover, he thought with a private smile. He pretended interest in the notes to hide the light he was sure would show in his eyes, while the old lady prattled innocently on.

'Shame she had to go back to work so soon, though. That babe can't be more than a few months old, I don't suppose, but times change, doctor. It wasn't so very long ago she wouldn't have been able to hold her head up in the street, and yet now—well, to tell the truth, we all think the world of her, baby or no baby. No sign of the father, mind. Terrible the way some men shirk their responsibilities, isn't it?'

'Quite,' Oliver agreed with studied casualness, flipping the notes shut and standing up. 'OK, Mrs Bright, I'll see you this afternoon. And don't worry, we'll soon have you back to normal. Thank you, Sister.' He thrust the notes back into her hand, and turned on his heel.

Somehow he found the gap in the curtains and made his way out of the ward, down the corridor and back to his office without incident; then he went in, shut the door quietly, and slumped against it while he struggled to control his breathing.

Slowly the shock and disbelief gave way to a merciless, white-hot rage. He tortured himself with the memory of their lovemaking, the beauty of her body stretched naked and unashamed beneath him, the silken warmth of her surrounding him, welcoming him; the way she had clung to him, sobbing, while his frenzied thrusts had driven them both to madness and beyond; and then he pictured her with another man, laughing up at him with those same love-drenched grey eyes, opening her heart and her body to someone else—oh, God!—when she belonged to him.

The rage turned to pain, and twisted in his gut like a living thing, leaving him breathless and afraid; and then even that faded, and in its wake came a terrible, consuming grief. Oblivious to the ringing of the phone on his desk, he rolled his face to the wall and slammed his fist against the plaster. His body started to shake violently and, like a wild thing, a single, terrible sob clawed at his throat and fought its way free.

He clamped down on it, and gradually the shaking receded to a faint tremor. Taking great care with his breathing, he moved to his desk and picked up the still-ringing phone.

*   *   *

For Bron, the next few days were misery. She saw Oliver briefly with a patient on Tuesday, and he was curt and distant; when their eyes met across the patient, his contained such a mixture of anger and contempt that she stepped back in dismay, knocking over a trolley of instruments.

By the time she had cleared them up, he had arranged for the patient's admission and left the department.

She didn't see him again until Thursday night, again over a patient, and this time she followed him as he strode away.

'Oliver? Oliver, please, talk to me!'

He ignored her and strode swiftly on, so that she had to run to keep up, and finally she grabbed his arm and yanked him round to face her.

'Talk to me!' she pleaded.

'About what?'

She swallowed. There was a murderous light in his eyes, and, behind it, such utter desolation that her heart stalled briefly. 'About whatever it is that's turned you into an angry stranger. . .'

His eyes flicked over her contemptuously, reducing her to silence. His voice—that sensuous, gravelly voice that had poured over her like warm honey—was coldly sarcastic. 'How did it happen, Bron? At a conference, perhaps? Or maybe in a resident's room, passing the time between calls?'

She felt the blood drain from her face. 'I don't know what you mean,' she whispered.

'Oh, yes, you do!' Did you imagine I wouldn't find out?' Now his voice was like chips of ice, cold and sharp, and yet in it she could hear the terrible pain.

How had he found out? 'Bron, why didn't you tell me?' he whispered hoarsely.

'Oh, Oliver, I was going to tell you the night of the ball, but the fireworks——'

'How convenient,' he sneered. 'It doesn't wash, Bron. You deceived me, quite deliberately.'

'No!' she cried, but his savage glare reduced her to quivering silence yet again. When he spoke, each word was given brutal emphasis.

'Did you or did you not deliberately conceal from me the existence of your child?'

Beneath the burning cobalt of his eyes, she felt her heart shrivel and die. She closed her eyes and dropped her head forward. She couldn't lie to him. 'Yes,' she whispered.

'Thank you,' he said quietly. 'At last you're being honest. Now, if you'll excuse me, I have a patient waiting.'

'Oliver, no, we have to talk!'

He turned back to her with a look of such withering scorn that she stopped in her tracks. 'I have nothing left to say to you,' he rasped, and, turning on his heel, he walked briskly away.

'You don't understand!' she cried, but he turned the corner and left her there, tears streaming down her face, oblivious of the curious glances of the hospital staff hurrying about their business in the quiet of the hospital night.

It was Jesus who found her, who led her gently back to her room and brought her a cup of coffee and held her while she cried; Jesus who dealt with the next patient and then came back and tucked her up in bed and sat with her until sleep claimed her; and when she woke, it was to find that he had guarded over her all night, dealing with all the emergencies and ensuring that she was not disturbed.

When Jim came in, Jesus found him and told him what had happened, and he sent her home.

Her mother was horrified to see her looking so bereft, and held her close, but the tears refused to fall, and Bron thought she would never feel again.

Her father sent her to bed and watched over her, and somehow she got through the weekend without dying, although she didn't know how. She felt as if everything inside had flown apart and was whirling round, fragments of heart and soul and conscience all battering against her mind.

She was listless and withdrawn, and Livvy, for once, was content simply to sit on her knee and rest her head against her mother's breast, as if she sensed the terrible pain inside.

She got through the next week somehow, preferring to work although Jim had told her to take time off, and somehow the humanity of her patients and the silent support of the staff bolstered her so that she was able to cope.

As the weeks went by, so she saw Oliver occasionally around the hospital, and began to realise how much he had dropped by before without really needing to.

She started to function again as a person as well as a doctor, and one day she was even heard to laugh with one of the patients. Kathleen and Jim exchanged a look of relief, and everything settled back to normal.

Everything, that was, except Friday lunchtimes. Bron refused to go to the pub again, and, despite Jim's assurances that Oliver wouldn't be there, she refused his invitations and instead brought sandwiches in every day, avoiding the dining-room as well.

Livvy was growing and, as the summer drew to a close, Bron took her shopping in Norwich for new clothes ready for the winter. They didn't have time to find a coat, so Elizabeth said she would take her again some time and have a look.

On Saturdays Bron did the shopping, and once she bumped into Oliver in the supermarket, just as she was loading a huge bag of disposable nappies into her trolley.

Pain flared in his eyes, but he stamped it down, greeted her coolly and left without his purchases. Bron could have wept for him. Why was he so angry? He had refused to discuss it with Jesus, shutting his friend out so effectively that he had ceased to try to get through to him.

Dispirited, she returned home, and passed the rest of the weekend trapped inside her head with her melancholy thoughts. Her parents were seriously worried, and even considered contacting Oliver, but Bron forbade it, and they respected her decision, against their better judgement.

She looks like hell, he thought, as he wandered aimlessly in the park. Her eyes were haunted with a dreadful sadness, and she was much thinner than before. He sat on a bench near the scene of the firework disaster, and closing his eyes he pictured her there, her eyes filled with helpless rage as she calmly tended to her patients, biting her lip to stop from crying with them when the pain became too much to bear, joking and encouraging to help the less badly injured cope with the long wait for transport.

She had been magnificent, a true professional, and he loved her, despite her unfaithfulness.

A frown creased his brow. Unfaithfulness was a strange word to use, he thought, and tried to imagine what she must have felt when she had heard about Tom's death and believed that he was married. The very thought of their situations being reversed sent an unseen knife twisting in his gut, and he breathed in sharply to control the pain.

But, if she had believed that he was married, was it so wrong for her to have sought solace elsewhere? Could he really blame her for drowning her sorrows and exorcising his ghost in the arms of another man? If the baby was only a few months old, as that gossipy old woman had said, then she had presumably waited at least six months before—oh, God, he really didn't want to think about her getting pregnant in another man's arms; but he made himself face it head on, and remembered another thing old Mrs Bright had said— that there was no sign of the father. So he had deserted her, too?

He closed his eyes and, despite his terrible, aching jealousy, he felt a tidal wave of pity for the fragile, wonderful girl he had met at the conference. She had been so spontaneous and warm, full of life and vigour, not afraid to test the strength of the amazing feelings that had struck them without warning, and yet, because of a single word out of place, the world had come crashing down around her ears.

God, why hadn't he written sooner? He thought of the endless hours beside Tom's cot, willing him to live, and knew that he hadn't written to Bron because he had had nothing left to spare for any other human being at that time. There had been time to write but, as he'd sat beside the tiny baby fighting for life, it had seemed to Oliver that, if he could channel his energy and life-force into that fragile little body, then Tom would survive. So he hadn't written until Tom was two months old and obviously thriving, and he had felt at last that there was time to do things other than sit and pray and offer succour.

No, he couldn't change the past, but the future was still accessible to him, and he didn't have to let his jealous rage ruin her life and his. So she had had an affair—so what? So had he, plenty of them—but not since her. No matter, he told himself. And a child was a child, and needed love. It was at least half Bron's, and, as such, lovable, without any of the endearing little characteristics that had enabled Tom to wind his uncle round his little finger.

Oliver missed them. Clare had married Antonio and left for Sardinia two weeks ago. The toys had been packed away, and the house seemed sterile and empty. It would be good to hear a child's happy laughter echoing round its walls again.

The decision made, he stood up, a trace of warmth and hope flickering in his eyes, and headed back towards the house with a spring in his stride and a lift to his head that had been absent for weeks.

It was time to ask Bronwen to marry him—if she would have him. His stride faltered, and then strengthened. Now was not the time for doubts.

*   *   *

Monday dawned with a chill in the air.

'I'll take her to Norwich today and get that coat,' Elizabeth Jones said over breakfast, and Bron nodded.

'Thanks. Look out for some corduroy dungarees, too, if you get a chance. I must dash, I'll be late. Bye, sweetheart——' Bron bent to kiss the sticky little upturned face and, grabbing her keys and bag, ran for the door.

A and E was busy, which suited Bron. All she could see in a moment of quiet was Oliver's haunted eyes, so the fewer quiet moments in each day the better.

At half-past eleven, a minor lull gave her time for a quick cup of coffee, and she headed for the staff-room.

'You just missed Oliver,' Mick O'Shea told her. 'He was looking mighty pleased with himself, I must say.'

Bron wondered if he had found out that Livvy was his—because he had obviously, she had later deduced, got the wrong end of the stick all those weeks ago and decided the child was someone else's. Maybe he had finally listened to Jesus.

She missed him again at lunchtime, and began to wonder if it wasn't all an elaborate hoax.

Then, at ten to five, when she was winding down ready to hand over, he appeared in Sister's office, still in his Theatre-greens, with an unfamiliar diffidence that sat awkwardly on his broad shoulders.

'May I have a word?' he asked quietly.

She avoided his eyes. 'Fire away,' she said, a little tersely because of her sudden nervousness.

'Is there somewhere more private we can go, where we won't be interrupted?'

Bron looked at him then, and the man she saw was a little grim-faced, slightly remote, a stranger.

She was about to refuse, and he realised that.

'Please?' he begged, and the slight tremor in his voice was her undoing.

'We'll borrow Jim's office, he's already gone,' she said, and led the way, trying to stop her knees from knocking together and her heart from breaking out of her ribs.

Once in there, she crossed to the window and stood, pretending interest in the landscaping of the gardens and ignoring Oliver's tense presence behind her.

'Look at me,' he commanded softly, and while her mind rebelled her body obeyed him, as it always had.

He was closer than she had realised, but still he made no move to touch her.

He stood silent for so long that she began to wonder if he had forgotten what he had to say.

'I want to apologise,' he began, eventually. 'I made you very unhappy the last time we really spoke, and I'm sorry. I remember telling you once, long ago, that I would never forgive myself if I hurt you. I didn't realise how true that was until just recently——'

Bron *was* hurt, and she was still hurting, and so she struck out blindly. 'Is that why you want to apologise? So you can forgive yourself? Well, fine, I accept your apology. Now leave me alone.'

'Please hear me out,' he said, and, when she nodded, he continued softly, 'I said some pretty unforgivable things, Bron, but I was hurting. A patient of your father's let it slip while we were talking one day, and I just went AWOL. Then, finally, I analysed my feelings.

'I realised that the way I felt, knowing that you had had someone's baby, was very much the way you must have felt when you thought I was married with a pregnant wife. Rage, jealousy, bitterness, betrayal—it made me see what you must have gone through. I had no right to hate you for taking another lover, or for trying to forget me. When I got over that—no, please let me say it all, then you can have your bit—I realised that, no matter what, I still love you. I think I always will, no matter what you decide.'

He paused, searching her face for something, and then, finding it, he took a deep breath and carried on.

'Bron, your baby needs a father, and you need someone to help you share the burden of parenthood. You need a friend, someone to laugh with and cry with, someone to share the responsibilities and the pain—and the long, lonely nights. You said you loved me——' he paused again, and his voice shook. '—I don't know if you can love me now, after what I've said and done to you, but, if you want me, Bron, I'm here for you. . .'

He closed his eyes and waited, a muscle twitching in his jaw, and she could see the tension in every line of his body.

'What are you saying, Oliver?' she asked, half afraid of the answer.

His eyes flew open and, in the second before he blanked it out, all the uncertainty and vulnerability was there for her to see.

'I'm asking you to marry me, and let me adopt your baby. I'm asking you to come and live with me as my wife. I know you'll probably need time to think but, if you want me, I'm here, and I love you. I was going to ask you before the fireworks exploded, but there wasn't time, and afterwards—afterwards, everything fell apart. If I've left it too late, I'm sorry. . .'

Slowly, from somewhere so deep inside her that she had forgotten it existed, joy bubbled up and flooded over, lighting her face and bringing tears of happiness to her eyes.

She lifted her hand to his face, and laid her palm against the rough satin of his jaw.

'Yes,' she breathed, 'oh, Oliver, yes!'

He moved then, closing the gap and crushing her to his chest with arms that shook with emotion. A shudder racked his body, and she could feel his heart pounding beneath her ear.

When she could speak, Bron eased away from him and looked up at his face, all the love in her heart written clearly for him to see.

'There's something you ought to know, before we go any further——'

'Bron, can you come?' Kathleen poked her head round the door. 'Sorry to break up the party, but we've got an RTA coming in, and it sounds pretty grim. In fact, can you come too, Oliver? There's a baby with massive internal injuries, and the paediatricians are all out or in Theatre, so I expect you'll end up with her.'

Immediately he was all business. 'How many others?' he asked as he went with Kathleen down the corridor. Bron straightened her shoulders, wiped the tears off her face and followed them. There was nothing she could do to remove the smile, however.

They prepared the trauma unit while Mick O'Shea finished dealing with the patient he was treating, and Bron checked the notes to see if there was anything urgent waiting. She told the people still waiting to be seen that there was an emergency coming in and that they would have an extended wait, and apologised, dealing with the one or two who got stroppy, with the patience of a saint, and then, just when one man was demanding to see the person in charge, the ambulances arrived and the injured were disgorged hastily and with enormous care.

The man blanched, closed his mouth and sat down quietly. Suppressing a smile, Bron turned on her heel and followed the trolleys through into the treatment area. She passed Oliver, bent over a tiny, silent child, and went on to assess the other patients.

Jim was back and dealing with the mother of the baby, who was unconscious but not, apparently, seriously injured, and Mick was arranging X-rays for two others with wrist and rib injuries. They had been driving, and the injuries were consistent with being flung forwards against a seatbelt and steering-wheel.

'Anyone know what happened?' Bron asked, as she examined the last casualty—a man called David Barrie, in his early thirties with a broken arm and splinters of glass in his face.

'It was my fault, apparently,' the man said, his voice rich with anguish. 'I don't know what happened. One minute I was driving along towards Norwich, and the next minute I woke up in the car, on the wrong side of the road, with a killer headache and stuffed full of broken glass.'

Bron frowned. 'Can't you remember anything about it?'

'Only the shadows. Flickering, you know. There's an avenue of trees, and the sun was coming in sideways; it was all I could see—the sun flickering, on, off, on, off. . .then it all went blank.'

'And you woke up with a headache?'

He nodded slightly, and winced. 'That's right. I wasn't going fast. More than my job's worth to speed. I can't understand it. . .'

He trailed off with a groan, and Bron sprayed his face with a freeze aerosol and started to pick glass out of the skin with tweezers.

'Just lie as still as you can; that's it. I'll get your face sorted out while we're waiting for X-ray.' After a while, she sat up and straightened her spine. 'OK, that's all out now.' She swabbed it down with antiseptic and sprayed it again with plastic skin to protect the tiny cuts from infection, then she turned her attention to his earlier remarks. 'What is it you do for a living?'

'I'm a policeman,' he murmured, and Bron raised her eyebrows.

'Oh. Tell me, David—have you ever had a fit?'

'What, like epilepsy, you mean?' She nodded, and he shook his head in denial. 'No, never. Why?'

Bron shrugged. 'Just something you said about the light. Sometimes convulsions can be brought on by flickering light—strobes, video games, things like that. Maybe I'm wrong, but I would say you've probably had some kind of epileptic attack—maybe minor, perhaps more major. There are several types, and it's often brought on by stress, as well. I think it would be worth looking into. Just hang on a minute and I'll see if we can get your X-ray done, then we'll get a plaster on that arm and have you in for twenty-four hours for observation. Maybe they'll run some tests.'

He stopped her as she was leaving the cubicle. 'Doctor? Do you think you could find out how the others are? I feel so responsible——'

She came back to his side and gave his uninjured

hand a reassuring squeeze. 'David, I don't think it can have been your fault. But I will go and ask for you. Is there anyone you want me to contact?'

He shook his head. 'No—there's no one. Not any more.' He turned his face away, and she withdrew to give him privacy. Whatever had happened in the past was still hurting him, and he obviously didn't want to talk about it. She wondered how stressful it had been, and whether or not it had contributed to his fit, if he had had one. She checked on X-ray, and was told her patient would be next, and then wrote up his notes so far and went to find out how the others were progressing.

The two drivers with fractures were in the plaster-room being strapped up prior to being sent home, and two others who had been brought in a later ambulance had had minor running-repairs and were on their way home. That left the mother and baby.

Jim stuck his head out of the trauma unit as she went past, and called to her quietly.

'This lady keeps saying, "Find Bron—you must get Bron." Do you know her?'

Bron looked past him into the treatment-room, and her heart lurched in her chest. 'Mum! Oh, God, Jim, it's my mother!' She crossed quickly to her mother's side and took her hand, pressing it against her face.

'Mum—Mum, it's Bron. You're going to be OK. We'll look after you. I'll phone Dad. Don't worry. Everything's going to be fine.'

Her mother's eyes flickered open, and she seemed to stare straight through her daughter for a moment, then she focused and her fingers tightened on Bron's.

'Livvy!' she said in anguish, and Bron's legs turned to jelly.

From somewhere inside she found a voice, and was amazed to find it was so normal.

'She's fine. Don't worry. I'm going to see her now. Hang on, Mum. I love you——' Her voice cracked, and she dropped a light kiss on her mother's bruised cheek and turned away.

Her eyes were wide and sightless, and Jim took one look at her and led her, unresisting, from the room.

'Where is she? Where's my daughter?' Her voice was calm and controlled, and she clamped down on the urge to cry.

'In Theatre. Kathleen and I signed the consent forms.'

'How is she?'

Jim ran his huge hand through his tangled hair and searched round desperately for inspiration. He saw Jesus walking towards them, and Kathleen in the distance on the telephone. Nothing—nothing that would help, that would make this any easier to say, or easier to bear.

'She's very seriously injured, Bron. It seems she had a toy tucked into the straps of her car seat, and with the force of the impact. . .' He took a deep breath, and switched into his professional voice. 'Her spleen's ruptured, maybe her bowel as well. There might be damage to her lungs, but that's less likely. There were no fractures, but she's got a bump on the side of her head, probably from being flung back against the seat as they came to rest, and she's probably slightly concussed. She's lost a lot of blood.'

Jesus joined them, and shot a quick glance from one to the other. 'Problems?'

Jim nodded. 'Her daughter.'

Bron turned anguished eyes up to Jesus and reached blindly for his hand. The warmth and comfort flowing out from it helped her to ask the next question.

'Jim, is she—will she die?'

He swallowed hard. 'I don't know. She's in the best hands. If she can be saved, then Oliver will save her.'

Bron felt as if fingers of ice had crawled over her skin. 'No!' she whispered. 'Jim, he can't——'

'Why?'

'Because she's his daughter,' Jesus said quietly, and caught Bron as she crumpled.

CHAPTER TEN

OLIVER'S face over the green mask was impassive, controlled. In front of him, the tiny child was lying unconscious. She was draped in green, only the small, bruised abdomen visible. Her mop of blonde curls was contained by a cap, and a mask covered her face.

At her head sat the anaesthetist, checking monitors and waiting. Finally he nodded. 'OK. She's as stable as I can get her. She's all yours.'

Oliver nodded his thanks, and closed his eyes. Please, God, don't let me bungle this, he thought, and took a steadying breath.

Then he opened his eyes, held out his hand palm up, and wrapped his fingers around the scalpel. 'Here goes,' he muttered under his breath, and then louder, 'Get ready with the suction, please.'

On the other side of the table, his registrar stood by with retractors, and between them they exposed the damage.

'What a bloody mess!' the younger man said, and Oliver raised an eyebrow.

'Bowel's gone. Suction, please, I can't see what I'm doing.'

Working as quickly as possible, he clamped off the blood supply to the spleen, to arrest the haemorrhage, and then inspected the tear in the bowel wall. It was only small, and he sutured it quickly, then turned his attention back to the spleen.

'You'll have to remove it, won't you?' the reg. said doubtfully.

'Not if I can help it,' Oliver replied grimly.

It was slow work, and twice they had to pause and wait while the baby's blood-pressure faltered and then recovered.

'I'll have to bring her up a bit,' the anaesthetist said, and Oliver frowned.

'OK, if you must. I'm not finished, by a long way, though.'

The anaesthetist nodded and adjusted the knobs slightly. 'Have we got any more blood for her?'

The nurse nodded. 'No more B neg, but we're getting more from Cambridge, and we've got some O neg if we have to use it.'

She wiped the sweat from Oliver's brow, and watched as his skilful hands carefully excised the portions of spleen that were too badly damaged to be repaired. 'How does it look?' she asked.

'Grim. I may be able to save the pedicle, but the rest was shot to hell. We'll have to get some antibiotics into her to prevent peritonitis from the bowel leak if she lives that long. Have we got any ID on her yet?'

'Don't think so—oh, hang on. Jean's just arrived.'

The junior theatre-nurse hurried over to the door, spoke briefly and returned to the table. 'Her name is Olivia Jones, age nineteen months. Her mother's a registrar here, apparently.'

The scalpel landed on the floor with a harsh, metallic clatter that was shocking in the quiet room, and over the mask Oliver's face went chalk-white. He swore, quietly but explicitly.

Olivia?

Dimly he was conscious of everyone's eyes on him, but all he could see was the wild tangle of golden curls, and the face that was so like Tom's. He hadn't seen it before—he wished to God he hadn't seen it now.

'Mr Henderson—Oliver, are you all right?'

'What did you say her blood-group was?'

His voice was hoarse, and over his head the theatre team exchanged puzzled glances.

'B neg.'

His. The rarest, and the final piece in the puzzle. He lowered his eyes to his child, and squeezed his lids shut to stop the tears.

'Her BP's falling,' the anaesthetist warned, and the professional in him gathered together and took over.

'Sutures,' he said quietly, and, with hardly a tremor in his hands, he carried on. Finally the repair was complete, and he loosened the artery forceps.

His shoulders sagged with relief. The haemorrhage had been successfully halted.

'Well done, sir,' his registrar said with quiet respect.

'Everything accounted for?'

'Scalpel missing,' the nurse said.

'On the floor,' he said tersely. 'OK, I'll close her up. How is she now?'

'Stable again. You may just have got away with it, you lucky bastard.'

He winced inwardly at the word. Technically speaking, if he had pulled this off, she was the lucky bastard. He brought the edges of the wound together with great care, using a cosmetic suture, and when he had finished he stood back and stripped off his gloves, then tugged down his mask and walked with them through to Recovery.

He watched as the nurses shifted her to her side and brought her slowly back to consciousness, and, as her eyes fluttered open, his heart wrenched in his chest, because they were his eyes, staring straight at him.

He felt a great roaring in his ears and, reaching out, he grasped her tiny hand and folded it in his own. Then, crouching down, he laid a feather-light kiss on her cheek, and smoothed the hair back tenderly from her little face. 'Hello, sweetheart,' he murmured softly, for her ears only. 'Everything's going to be all right. You'll see. I'll get Mummy now. Love you, treasure.'

He straightened up and eyed his staff, who were all watching him with curious expressions.

'Thank you, all, that was a brilliant effort. Well done.' He swallowed. His voice was gravelly and raw with emotion. 'We might just have saved my daughter's life.'

He left them rooted to the spot, and, thrusting open the doors, he all but ran down to A and E, to the mother of his child.

It was the longest three hours of Bron's life. She had stayed with her mother until her father arrived, then gone back to Mr Barrie and seen to his admission. He had gripped her hand and asked her about the others, and she had replied mechanically.

'And the baby?' he pressed.

'She's in Theatre now.'

'I hope to God she lives,' he said fervently, and Bron squeezed her lips shut and nodded distractedly. 'I didn't mean to hurt anyone. I can't understand what happened. If she dies, I'll never forgive myself.'

Somehow Bron found her voice, and smoothed his brow with her hand. 'Don't blame yourself, David. It wasn't your fault. You couldn't help it——'

'But if she dies——'

'Don't! Don't say that!' Bron's composure shattered, and she turned blindly away, stumbling into the corridor. She passed Mick, and he went in to Mr Barrie and took over from her, soothing the distressed man and reassuring him.

Bron walked unsteadily down to the staff-room and went in. Jesus and Jim Harris were both there, and turned to her as she entered.

'Any news?' she asked, and they shook their heads. She sat down facing the door, and Jim gave her a cup of coffee and stood over her while she drank it.

'It's foul, Jim—I hate sugar in it!'

'You need it. Eat something——' He thrust a plate of sandwiches under her nose, and her stomach heaved.

'No, I couldn't. Please, Jim?'

He put the sandwiches down and sat beside her, his large hand covering her knee. 'We'll wait with you,' he said softly, and he squeezed her knee gently.

'Thank you.'

They sat for half an hour, and then Bron leapt up and started pacing. The two men exchanged helpless shrugs.

Mick poked his head round the door. 'Someone here's put her hand through the patio doors, Jim. Can you help me sew her up? It's a bit tricky.'

Bron jumped at it. 'Let me, please. I can't just sit here with nothing to do—let me do it, Jim?'

'Are you sure you're up to it?' he asked, and she nodded.

'I'll be fine—I just can't sit here and wait for—any more.'

She shoved her hands into her coat-pockets to steady them, and followed Mick down the corridor. Once in the treatment-room, her professional self took over and, as she swabbed and sutured and chatted, she forced her personal worries aside and concentrated on bringing order to the chaos under her hands.

'How did it happen?' she asked, and the woman gave Bron a twisted little smile.

'I fell over the dog. She loves to be near me, and I forgot. I turned round and walked across the conservatory—only she was lying right behind me! Luckily I had my gardening-gloves on.'

'Yes, it was lucky,' Bron agreed. 'All your major blood vessels, nerves and tendons are OK. It could have been much worse.'

Eventually she straightened and smiled at the woman. 'There. You'll be fine in a couple of weeks. You'll have some scarring, but I've done my best with the sutures. It shouldn't be too bad.'

'I'll kill that dog,' the woman said with a rueful smile, and Bron chuckled.

'Always underfoot, aren't they? Take care, now. You'll need to come back in a week to have those stitches out, and meanwhile look where you're going!'

'Thanks, dear. Bless you.'

Bron left her with the nurse, and made her way back to the staff-room, and as she did so her fears came back to haunt her with full force.

'Anything?'

They shook their heads, and then they heard footsteps, coming hard and fast down the corridor, and Oliver appeared in the doorway. His face was taut with emotion; his eyes were red-rimmed, and a muscle worked in his jaw. His lips were pressed firmly together, and there was a white line around them. He looked exhausted.

As he saw Bron, he hesitated, and she felt her fear rise up like bile. Her hand clutched her throat, and her lips parted, but she couldn't speak—couldn't say the words that could take all meaning from her life.

Then he smiled, and the harsh glitter in his eyes softened and warmed; he opened his arms, and she flew into them, accepting the wordless comfort of his embrace.

'She's fine,' he murmured into her hair, 'she's fine, darling. Don't worry. It's all over now. She's fine. She's. . .'

His grip tightened, and Bron hugged him back, relief numbing her for a moment, and then the words came, tumbling over themselves to be spoken now.

'Oliver, I have to tell you—about Livvy—you shouldn't have done that, I should have told you——'

'Shh. Bron, it's all right, I know.' His arms tightened convulsively around her, and he pressed his lips against her hair. 'She's in Recovery now. She's going to be fine. Her spleen was smashed to bits, but I've managed to save enough of it, I think, and we found a tiny tear in her bowel, but she'll be fine, darling, really, she'll be fine——'

His voice cracked, and he buried his face in Bron's hair and let the reaction overtake him.

Behind him, they heard the door click quietly shut behind Jim and Jesus, their vigil over.

After a while, when she could speak again, Bron mumbled against his chest, 'When did you realise?'

He led her to the chairs and sat down abruptly, tugging her on to his lap and wrapping her in his arms.

'I'd just finished sorting her out and I was about to close her up when they said who she was. God, Bron, you even named her after me——'

He took a deep, shuddering breath, and she cupped his cheek in her hand and kissed him gently.

'How did you cope?'

He shook his head. 'I never want to go through that again. Thank God she didn't die, Bron—I would never have forgiven myself.'

She thought of Mr Barrie, and her mother saying she should have left Norwich earlier, and should have realised she had tucked the doll into her straps, and how Bron had berated herself for not getting the coat the previous week, and she smiled ruefully. 'If you wanted to take the blame, you'd have to get in the queue! There are a lot of us there already. I'm just so sorry you had to find out like that. I was about to tell you, in Jim's office, but Kathleen came in and all hell broke loose. It's happened every time. I tried to tell you before, but the fireworks went up, and then again after Mrs Bright let it out and you misunderstood, but you wouldn't let me—oh, darling!'

He hugged her, and gave her a funny, lop-sided little smile. 'You know, I'm surprised I didn't recognise her when I examined her. She's so like Tom, but I didn't really take it in. It was only when they said her name and age, and that she was your daughter, and then I found out her blood-group's the same as mine—I could have died.' Another shudder ran through him, and he buried his face against her breasts. 'You're right—it wasn't the best way to find out.'

'Did you hand over to your registrar?'

He shook his head. 'No. He can't sew as well as I can, and I thought, if I did nothing else for her, I could leave her with minimal scarring. There were no decisions to make any more, nothing that my judgement was required on. It's funny, I wouldn't have thought I could do it, but I didn't have the choice, and of course I don't know her——'

'Oh, darling! That's all going to change——'

'Starting now. Come on, let's go and see her.'

He stood up and lifted Bron to her feet, and then, putting his arm round her waist and tucking her firmly into his side, he led her up to Recovery.

The theatre staff were still milling around, and they fell into embarrassed silence when Bron and Oliver came into the room.

'Don't mind us,' he said with a wry grin, and led Bron over to the tiny hump under the bedclothes. She was a mass of tubes and wires, and Bron's heart lurched, even though she was used to it.

She thought, It doesn't make any difference how often you see it, when it's your child, it hurts. Oliver was speaking to her again, his voice steady beside her.

'We'll keep her here for a while, just to be on the safe side.' He turned back to the registrar. 'Any B neg arrived?'

He nodded, and tipped his head to one side. 'Did you mean what you said, about her being your daughter?'

Oliver smiled slowly. 'Yes, I meant it.' He turned back to Bron, and tenderly wiped the tears from her cheeks. 'Don't cry, darling. She'll be fine.'

'She looks so frail and tiny. . .'

Oliver bit his lip and gripped Bron's hand. 'She'll make it. She's got her father's determination and her mother's courage.'

'Don't you mean pig-headedness?' she sniffed with a tearful smile.

'No, I don't, I mean courage.' He reached out a large hand and brushed it lightly over the pale, downy cheek. His voice was hushed and reverent. 'She's beautiful, Bron. I love her already. I feel we've come through together. Can you understand that?'

Bron squeezed his other hand. 'Oh, yes,' she whispered.

They sat with Livvy for two hours, and then went with her down to the paediatric unit. She was sleeping peacefully, her tiny fist curled under her cheek, and they watched her in silence as she slept.

'Have I thanked you for saving her life?' Bron said eventually, and Oliver made a choked sound and gripped her hand.

'Don't be bloody silly!'

'I mean it. Without her, what have I got left?'

'Me?'

She turned to him, and searched his face. 'Can you ever forgive me for keeping it from you?'

He gave a slight, shaky laugh. 'I'm working on it. Bron, I know why you did it, and I know I didn't make it easy for you to tell me. Right now, all I want to do is crawl into a corner and lick my wounds.'

'Mind if I come too?' she asked tentatively, and he shook his head.

'You're welcome,' he said softly.

The paediatrician, Peter Travers, came in and had a quiet word with them, then lifted the covers to inspect the incision.

'Very neat,' he said, but all Bron could see was a line a mile long cutting her daughter in half, and she turned her face into Oliver's shoulder with a little whimper. 'Do I believe all these rumours that are flying around?' Peter continued, one eyebrow raised slightly.

Oliver chuckled. 'I'll put a notice on the bulletin board, shall I? "Bronwen Jones and Oliver Henderson are pleased to announce the survival of their daughter, Olivia." How's that?'

'Oh, very droll. Take the lady home, Henderson. She's out on her feet. We'll ring you if there's the slightest change, or if she wakes up. Go and get some sleep, both of you.'

He turned away, and Oliver looked at Bron. 'Coming home?'

She nodded. It sounded wonderful.

They walked hand in hand through the hospital corridors, leaving a trail of bemused hospital staff in their wake. Bron didn't notice, and Oliver didn't care. He had more important things to think about.

He opened the car door for her, and Bron settled back against the soft grey leather with a sigh. Home, she thought. Did he really ask me to marry him? Does he really know about Livvy? And did it really happen?

She closed her eyes and drifted off into an exhausted doze, and in her dreams she felt the warm hardness of a pair of strong arms lifting her, cradling her against the safety of a firm chest. She could hear a heartbeat, slow and steady, under her ear, and snuggled against it with a tiny, satisfied sigh.

When she woke, she was alone in the bedroom, and the light was on in the adjoining bathroom. She could hear water running, so she slipped her legs over the side of the bed and went to investigate.

Oliver was standing at the basin, naked except for a towel round his waist, shaving. 'Hi,' he said softly, and she stepped up to him and laid her head against his shoulders. His skin was like hot satin, smooth and soft and taut over the easy ripple of his muscles as he moved, and she wrapped her arms around his waist and made a contented little noise in her throat.

'You sound like a cat,' he chuckled.

'Mmm,' she agreed, and dragged her nails over his taut abdomen.

He ducked away from her and wiped his face. 'I've run you a bath,' he said. 'Get in and I'll bring you supper.'

'In the bath?'

'Don't argue, just do it.'

She sketched a little salute, and he whacked her bottom on the way past. She heard him murmur, 'Sassy little minx!' as he went into the bedroom, and, with a smile playing around her lips, she closed the door and undressed quickly. The water was just right—hot enough to catch her breath, but cold enough—just!— to lower herself into with care.

She lay back with a sigh of relief, and let the hot water lap relaxingly round her shoulders. There was a thin layer of bubbles on the surface—not film-star style, but enough to shelter her a little from Oliver's eyes.

Silly though it was, she felt shy with him. This would be the first time he had seen her naked without the benefit of passion, and she was ridiculously conscious of the slight bulge of her tummy and the almost unnoticeable loss of tone of her breasts—all changes, she reminded herself, due to his daughter; and with the thought of Livvy came the tears that she had held back for so long.

She lay unmoving while the salty tears tracked down her cheeks and dripped off her chin, her chest lifting with the tiny sobs that shook her.

Then warm arms enfolded her and her head was cradled against a loving shoulder, and the sobs grew and then faded, leaving her listless and empty.

Oliver eased away from her and, without speaking, he helped her to her feet and lathered his hands. Then he washed her like a child, tenderly and thoroughly and without haste, and rinsed her before helping her out of the bath.

He wrapped her in a huge, warm towel and lifted her into his arms, laying her finally on the bed, then he knelt beside her and, freeing one end of the towel, he patted her gently dry. Through it all his hands were the impersonal hands of a doctor—gentle, thorough, but remote. She needed more. Now, in the aftermath of their private holocaust, she needed much, much more.

'Oliver?' she whispered, and his eyes met hers and held. 'Hold me—touch me—I need you. . .'

She saw something come to life in his eyes, a wild shiver of elemental male, and then he lowered his lids and his gaze swept over her body like a scorching tide.

There was nothing remote or impersonal about him now. She felt the tremor run through him, and held out her arms.

He came to her with a wild savagery and a frenzied desperation matched only by her own, and, as their bodies joined, Bron felt as if their souls had merged as well, so that it was impossible to tell where one finished and the other began.

When it was over and they lay tangled together, she slept, conscious only of the warmth of his body and the nearness of his soul.

The phone woke them at six, and, as Bron struggled to sit up, she heard Oliver replace the receiver on the bedside table and turn back to her.

'She's fine. She's just beginning to stir, and they think she's going to wake up soon. Shall we go?'

All through that day, Oliver appeared by her side with astonishing frequency.

'Are you getting any work done today?' she asked him as he dropped in for the fourth time that morning.

He chuckled. 'Only what I have to. I want to spend time with my wife and child.'

'I'm not your wife yet!'

His eyes met hers, full of warmth and love, and he smiled. 'In everything but name. You couldn't mean more to me than you do now. How's Livvy?'

They looked at the little scrap lying dozing in her cot, and Bron felt a tug in the region of her heart.

'She's been awake and spoken to me. Her tummy hurts a bit, and she refused to drink anything, but I suppose that's natural.'

Oliver nodded. 'It's the anaesthetic. Has Travers written her up for anything for the pain?'

'Aren't you dealing with her now?'

'Are you kidding? I can't, darling—I'm much too close.'

She sighed. 'I suppose so—it's just that I trust you.'

Oliver laughed softly. 'I'm sure Peter would be really flattered to hear you talking like that. He's a good man, Bron. He knows what he's doing.'

Bron tried to smile, but all she managed was a queer, lop-sided little twist. 'I keep telling myself she'll be all right, but——'

'Darling, she's fine. She's over the hump. They'll take the drip down later, and her drain will come out tomorrow. Children heal at the rate of knots. You'll see. Are you staying with her tonight?'

'Yes. I suppose I should go home and get some things. Have you seen Mum?'

He nodded. 'She's going home later. Her concussion seems to be very mild, and apart from her bruises she's perfectly OK. Her chest's a bit sore from hitting the seatbelt, but it could have been a hell of a lot worse.'

'What about the driver—David Barrie?'

'Ask Jesus, he's dealing with him. He said something about epilepsy. They're running some tests today, I think. If I come up at lunchtime to sit with her, you can go and get your stuff.'

A little frown creased Bron's brow, and Oliver's lips tightened.

'Bron, I've been shut out enough. I know why, and I can accept it, but from now on I'm here for her, and she's going to learn to love me too. Please? Give me time with her. Let us make friends. It's very important to me.'

'Oh, Oliver!' she said quietly, 'I wasn't trying to shut you out. Of course I want you to know her. That's been the hardest part—wanting to see you together. I even brought her to the park once, hoping you would be there and that this whole farce would be over—that's when I saw Clare and Antonio together, and he was kissing her, the day before you told me she wanted to marry him. I can't tell you how glad I am that she's not your wife!'

Oliver's bleep called him then, so, with a promise to return at lunchtime, he dragged himself reluctantly away.

Jesus came up a little later, and gave her a hug and a peck on the cheek.

'How goes, little lady?'

She laughed. 'Not so bad. Thank God he knows now. I couldn't bear it any longer.'

'Is he angry?'

'I don't think so—sad, because he's missed so much, but I expect we'll have fun catching up on all the time we've lost.'

Jesus raised an eyebrow, and Bron blushed and laughed softly. 'Not like that, Jesus!'

'I wouldn't blame him,' he said with a grin. 'I don't suppose, in all the chaos of what's happened, you've given a thought for the driver of the vehicle that caused the accident?'

'David? Yes, I have. How is he?'

'Distressed. He's glad to know the baby's all right, but he's very upset. We've got the results of the scans and the EEG and so on. Looks like grand mal. You were clever to spot that.'

'It was the sun. He kept talking about the lights flickering as the car went past a row of trees—you know how it flickers? It must have triggered it. Will he lose his job?'

'As a copper?' Jesus shrugged. 'I don't know. He won't be able to drive, of course, and that's what he does—drives a patrol car—so it's bound to have some effect on him.'

'I hope not too much,' Bron sighed. 'He seems a nice man. Tell him Livvy's OK, won't you, and give him my regards?'

Jesus grinned. 'You're very forgiving, considering he nearly killed your daughter.'

'Life is just a game of Russian roulette, Jesus. He didn't. That's enough for me. Thanks to Oliver, she's still alive, and the quality of her life will be good. That's all I can ask for.'

Oliver returned at lunchtime, and, suppressing her misgivings, Bron went home and packed her things. Her mother was back, ensconced in her chair with a cup of tea and her husband dancing attendance.

They pounced on Bron as she walked through the door.

'How is she?'

'Making progress. I hate all the wires and tubes and things. Silly, isn't it? I spend all day sticking them in people, and then, because she's mine, I can't cope with it! How are you?'

Her mother gave a strained little smile. 'Oh, I hurt a bit here and there. Mainly in my conscience. I should never have let her have that doll in the back——'

'Oh, Mum, not you too! Everyone wants to take the blame! If I'd been at home like the mother I ought to be, it wouldn't have happened. If Oliver and I had had the sense we were born with, she would never have even existed. If, if, if. She's fine, and so are you.'

'And how are you?' her father asked.

Bron's face broke into a tired but deeply happy smile. 'I'm—fantastic.'

'Will you be coming home?'

She shook her head. 'No, I'm sleeping at the hospital with Livvy. . .'

'I meant afterwards, when she comes out of hospital. What will you do then?'

'You don't know, do you? I haven't had time to tell you; we're getting married——'

'Oliver told us, this morning,' her mother said. 'Bron, will you go home with him?'

She looked from her mother to her father, and back again. 'I think so. It's where I belong.' She found a funny lump in her throat that made it difficult to speak. 'I'll miss you, though. I'll never forget what you've done for me. . .'

Bron found herself wrapped in her father's arms. 'We'll miss you, too, love, but you're right. You belong with him, you and your child. I hope you're happy. You've had a rotten run of luck, and you deserve some happiness—all of you.' He pushed her away. 'Go and pack now. You must get back to Livvy.'

His eyes were suspiciously bright, but Bron didn't notice, because her vision was distinctly misty, too. Sniffing inelegantly, she grinned and headed for the stairs.

When she got back to the little side-ward, Oliver and

Livvy were playing peek-a-boo round the end of the cot, and Livvy was giggling like mad.

'Funny man!' she said with a giggle, and Oliver looked sheepish.

'Hello, darling. Get everything?'

'Except lunch! How's she been?'

'Perky as a parrot. We've had lots of fun, haven't we?'

Livvy nodded. 'Stay!' she piped imperiously, and Oliver sat down again.

'Can I take Mummy and go and get some lunch?'

Livvy eyed them, thoughtfully, and her thumb slid into her mouth. She rubbed her eyes with her other fist, and curled on to her side. 'Sleep now, Mummy.'

They stayed until she had fallen asleep, and then tiptoed away, hand in hand. Today Bron was conscious of the funny looks, and tried to detach herself from him, but he resisted.

'What's the matter, Bron?' he teased. 'Ashamed to be seen with me?'

'Not at all,' she said lovingly, 'I was just trying to protect your reputation.'

'I think having you by my side is doing wonders for my reputation. They thought I was a dry, boring old stick. Finding out that I have a past has been the highlight of the century for my firm!'

Bron chuckled. 'I've been getting some sly comments this morning from the A-and-E crew—they've slipped in from time to time and quizzed me on my ability to keep secrets!'

They picked up their lunches and made their way to a quiet corner of the dining-room. 'Bron, do you think you want to carry on working now?' Oliver asked.

Bron eyed him seriously. 'I haven't had a great deal of time to think about it. I would like to work, but maybe part-time. I miss Livvy, but I missed the hospital atmosphere, too. But when the next baby comes along. . .'

Oliver choked. 'Don't tell me you're pregnant!' he croaked when he could speak.

Bron collapsed in a giggling heap against him. 'No, not yet, she spluttered, 'but after last night. . .'

'Oh, my God. Why do you do that to me? I only have to look at you and all my common sense flies out of the window. You——' he pointed his fork at her menacingly '—are going on the Pill, because I can't trust myself to have any damned control over the situation otherwise.'

'If it isn't too late!'

'Is this a private conversation, or may we join you?'

They looked up at Jim and Jesus, and flushed like guilty adolescents.

Then Oliver threw back his head and laughed till the tears ran down his cheeks. Bron leaned weakly against him and wiped her eyes, then grinned at their colleagues.

'Excuse us. It's just reaction. Of course you can join us.'

'So what were you talking about?' Jesus asked.

'Er—how soon Bron's going to give up work.'

Jim frowned at her. 'Has he bullied you into retirement?'

'Not exactly. I said I'd stop when we had the next baby.'

'So it could be years?'

'Or months. We'll keep you posted.'

They excused themselves and left the dining-room, giggling again.

'That's what they were talking about,' Jesus said, and rolled his eyes.

'How's Lucy?'

Jesus coughed self-consciously. 'Would you believe—pregnant?'

Jim's bellow of laughter followed Bron and Oliver up the corridor.

Later that evening, a nurse wheeled a little folding bed into Livvy's room, and Bron made up the bed and then slipped into the bathroom to wash and change into her nightclothes. When she got back to the side-ward, Oliver was here, holding Livvy's hand and telling her a story.

'Did you wake her up?'

He grinned guiltily. 'Only to say goodnight. She's nearly off again.' He turned back to the sleepy babe and finished the story. 'The end,' he said emphatically.

''Gain,' she mumbled round her thumb.

'Tomorrow.'

'OK. Night-night.'

He stooped low over the cot and brushed his lips against her cheek.

'Night-night, sweetheart. Sleep well.'

By the time he straightened, her eyes had drifted shut, and she was asleep.

Oliver turned to Bron, and she felt suddenly self-conscious in her nightdress under his scorching gaze. 'You look very demure,' he said huskily, and pulled her into his arms. 'I'll miss you tonight. I love you so much, Bron.'

He tipped up her face and grazed her lips with his, and she gave a soft moan and leaned into him; then his mouth came down hard on hers, and she felt the blood roaring in her veins. Everything else receded in the tide of passion that engulfed them, but finally Oliver brought the kiss gently to a close, and held Bron tightly in his arms as their breathing slowed and their hearts settled to a steady rhythm.

Then he eased away and gave her a rueful smile. 'Not here, not now. But soon. I've got something for you—I meant to give it to you yesterday, but somehow it got overlooked!'

He fished around in his pockets and came up with a tiny leather box. Cupping it in the palm of his hand, he opened it to show Bron the delicate gold band set with diamonds. 'It was my grandmother's,' he said, and slipped it on to Bron's trembling finger.

'It's lovely!' she breathed, and flung her arms around his neck. 'Oh, Oliver, I can't believe I'm allowed to love you at last!'

'Just promise me you'll never stop,' he murmured.

'I haven't yet,' she answered, 'despite everything. I don't think I will now.'

The following Sunday, Bron and Oliver were sitting on the playroom floor in the paediatric ward helping Livvy pile bricks, when Elizabeth and David Jones came in.

'Hello, G'amma, hello, G'andad,' Livvy piped, and they smiled at Bron and Oliver.

'Recover fast, don't they?'

'Incredible. How are you doing, Mrs Jones?'

'Please call me Elizabeth. I'm fine—bit stiff still, but

that's *anno Domini* for you. Is she really as good as she looks?'

Oliver laughed. 'Better. She can keep going for hours. I thought Tom was bad, but she's unstoppable!'

Just then Livvy got up and ran across to Oliver, tugging on his hand.

'Swing!' she demanded.

'Please,' he reminded her gently.

'Please, Daddy!'

Oliver flushed, and his throat worked for a second, then he let Livvy pull him up and lead him through the door into the little garden.

It was a warm day as only autumn days could be, and Bron and her parents watched as Oliver lifted Livvy and placed her in the baby-swing.

'Higher,' she shrilled, and they heard his answering murmur.

'Please, Daddy!' she piped obediently, and his smile made the sun seem pale by comparison.

'Sounds good, doesn't it?' Elizabeth said quietly, and Bron nodded.

'We're taking her home tomorrow,' she answered, and her heart filled with joy.

She heard Livvy shriek, 'More, Daddy!' and their laughter filled the air and floated round her like a warm sea. 'Mummy, come!' Livvy called.

Bron rose to her feet. Oliver lifted his daughter out of the swing and sat her on his hip, then he looked up and caught Bron's eye, and the current surged between them. Tomorrow, his eyes seemed to say, tomorrow. . .

Livvy grinned at her. 'Daddy pushed me high!'

'Yes, I saw,' she said.

'Cuddle, Mummy!'

'Yes, cuddle, Mummy,' Oliver echoed, and held out his other arm to her.

Her heart light, Bron stepped out into the sunshine of their smiles.

- MEDICAL ✚ ROMANCE -

The books for your enjoyment this month are:

MEDICAL DECISIONS Lisa Cooper
DEADLINE LOVE Judith Worthy
NO TIME FOR ROMANCE Kathleen Farrell
RELATIVE ETHICS Caroline Anderson

Treats in store!

Watch next month for the following absorbing stories:

ALL FOR LOVE Margaret Barker
HOMETOWN HOSPITAL Lydia Balmain
LOVE CHANGES EVERYTHING Laura MacDonald
A QUESTION OF HONOUR Margaret O'Neill

Available from Boots, Martins, John Menzies, W.H. Smith and other paperback stockists.

Also available from Mills and Boon Reader Service, P.O. Box 236, Thornton Road, Croydon, Surrey CR9 3RU.

Readers in South Africa — write to:
Independent Book Services Pty, Postbag X3010, Randburg, 2125, S. Africa.